POISONOUS PAWS

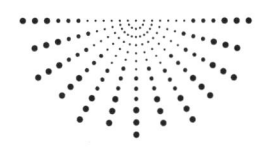

CEECEE JAMES

Copyright © 2021 by CeeCee James

All rights reserved.

No part of this book may be reproduced in any form or by any electronic or mechanical means, including information storage and retrieval systems, without written permission from the author, except for the use of brief quotations in a book review.

Cover by Mariah Sinclair

For my Family who puts up with a heck a lot of writer's shenanigans.

xxx

CONTENTS

Chapter 1	1
Chapter 2	11
Chapter 3	19
Chapter 4	24
Chapter 5	33
Chapter 6	42
Chapter 7	51
Chapter 8	55
Chapter 9	63
Chapter 10	68
Chapter 11	76
Chapter 12	82
Chapter 13	93
Chapter 14	101
Chapter 15	107
Chapter 16	112
Chapter 17	120
Chapter 18	128
Chapter 19	132
Chapter 20	141
Chapter 21	146
Chapter 22	153
Chapter 23	161
Chapter 24	165
Chapter 25	171
Chapter 26	176
Chapter 27	184
Chapter 28	191

Chapter 29	196
Chapter 30	203
Afterword	211

CHAPTER ONE

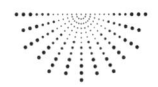

There should be a law that water pipes never be allowed to burst the first thing in the morning. Especially before anyone had a chance for a shower. Double the consequences if it happens on a Monday.

Like today, for instance. We hadn't even had a proper chance to grieve that the weekend was over, and now we had to weave through various buckets set about to catch the water dripping through the ceiling. The sound alone was enough to make anyone feel cranky, not to mention stinky armpits and hair twisted in a bun.

The summer storm showed no signs of lessening, and the fierce rain beat against the windows. Clouds gathered along the horizon like bullies waiting for a lonely kid to walk home from school. A dark mood hovered all around.

Cook's furrowing eyebrows reflected what we all felt. "Good gracious! Where's the grapefruit? And find the bottled water. I need to make the coffee!" she grumbled. She reached for the coffee grinder, and her foot connected with a pot and sent it spinning.

Naturally, Miss Janice didn't understand our predicament. She'd already directed Marguerite to call a plumber. In that light, the problem had already been solved, and she expected her breakfast with little delay.

They say when it rains it pours, and that sentiment seemed to seek every opportunity to be proven true as Lucy dropped the carton of eggs. Marguerite jumped at the noise only to turn and skid in the mess. One side of her wide hips rammed into the corner of the counter. The housekeeper's face turned purple as unspoken words remained sealed behind pressed lips.

"I'm so sorry!" Lucy said shakily. She had a slight lisp, and it really came out when she was excited or stressed. Like now. Her emotion was contagious, and I felt my own skin prickle.

"Good heavens. Now, what are we going to give the missus?" Cook asked. "No eggs, my word. And she's been in such a mood lately."

Cook stared into the refrigerator. After a moment, she said, "I'll do some nice oatmeal, toast, and Miss Janice's standard—half a ruby red grapefruit.

With that decided, we continued our morning chores serenaded by the rain-dinging-in-buckets concert. Perhaps the bad luck had declared a truce.

Until Cook discovered the missing grapefruit.

"Did you put it with the order I gave you?" Cook asked Lucy.

The poor girl swabbed the egg mess and shook her head. "I forgot. I'm sorry." She was not having a good day today.

"How could you forget? It was on the list." Cook scowled and directed her ire to Marguerite. "I swear if she tipped her head, a tumbleweed would roll out."

Marguerite swept by with a water bottle, her usual confidence having recovered from her injury. "Now, now. Don't be bad-mouthing my girls. Everything's fine. I've got this under control." She expertly wove around the splashing rain pots with grace as she moved to the counter. She shifted through the fruit in the bowl. "I'll simply tell Miss Janice that these oranges are exotic and specifically from Peru. That will impress her."

"Do oranges grow in Peru?" Mary asked.

"I hardly think this is the time to question that, now," the head housekeeper retorted and grabbed an orange.

She took it to the cutting board and in the process misjudged a pot. A splash landed on her foot, and her eyes closed.

"Here." From the floor, Lucy handed her a towel.

The front door knocker banged, and Butler answered it. Soon, the plumbers zigzagged their way through the carnage to survey the damage. Oranges were cut, coffee brewed, tea made, and something that resembled a fancy breakfast was pieced together on the silver tray. There was the Royal Albert china and Earl Grey tea, a plate with two slices of lightly toasted wheat bread with a tiny pot of fresh raspberry jam that Miss Janice insisted upon. Next to that was a small dish of homemade steamed granola with wild honey, a plate of sliced strawberries, and "Peru" orange segments.

Ducking around one of the plumbers, I plucked a rose from the centerpiece bouquet on the foyer pedestal and brought it back for a small crystal vase. Then, with the heavy silverware sitting on a cream-colored linen napkin and the daily newspaper tucked under my arm, I hoisted the tray and carefully carried it, china rattling and chattering, up to Miss Janice's bedroom.

Lightly, I tapped on her door.

"Come in," Miss Janice's voice could barely be heard above the noise of the rain pounding outside.

I opened the door and painstakingly made my way with the hefty tray over to the bedroom breakfast nook. Miss Janice sat in the bed, her slender frame wrapped in a floral silk wrapper and her steely gray hair pinned back from her face.

As she turned her head, I saw the pins sparkle in the incoming hallway light.

She twisted the switch on the bedside lamp and put on a pair of reading glasses in preparation for her morning newspaper. "If you could just bring that to me," she asked, beckoning with thin fingers adorned with rings that looked like gumball machine prizes in their gaudiness.

I deposited the tray and brought her the paper. Then I returned to set out the breakfast, starting with situating the plate neatly on the chintz tablecloth.

Miss Janice began to read, signaled by the happy crinkling of the paper being opened.

I placed the rose in the center of the table and the silverware next to the plate. I turned around to say, "I'm done, ma'am."

The words caught in my throat. Miss Janice sat with her mouth hanging open in an expression of horror.

Alarmed, I ran over. "Are you okay, ma'am? What's the matter?"

"It can't be!" she exclaimed, ignoring me and staring at the paper.

"Can't be what?" I asked.

"Look! It's him!" She jabbed a nude-polished manicured fingernail against the top headline of the newspaper.

In bold black letters, the headline screamed **Beloved City Founder Discovered Poisoned Behind Gas Station.**

By her reaction, I obviously deduced she knew him. "I'm so sorry."

"It says he hemorrhaged." She covered her face as a wail squeaked out, sounding like a strangled chicken. Immediately, I patted her shoulder in a rapid motion, half in panic. Before I could remind myself I wasn't trying to burp her, I half-screamed myself.

Something rose from the center of her bed. Finally it took the form of our orange-marmalade cat, Hank. He strode across to Miss Janice and sniffed her with his little nose. Her hand dropped from her face and rested on top of his head. Normally I would've been happy to see how they were making friends but the tears coursing down her face choked all the good feelings away.

I whispered. "Were you close?"

"He is our neighbor," she stammered. "Was. I was alone with him last night."

I must have gasped because she turned angry eyes at me. "Don't be a numbskull," she snapped. "We were both at the hotel gala. He sat across from me. In fact, my driver drove him home."

I nodded, slightly confused. People arrived at galas with drivers. They didn't need a ride home. She glanced at me and explained again. "Mr. Dee arrived with a friend, but apparently this person left without him."

She smoothed out the newspaper and read out loud the rest of the details. They were surprisingly few. Just that the coroner suspected poison and the police would be contacting all the suspects and interested parties soon.

When she finished, she sighed and glanced over at her food. "I suppose I should eat something."

I didn't want to break it to her about the grapefruit, and she didn't seem to notice. Absentmindedly, she stroked Hank's head and then became aware of him.

"How did you get in here?" she asked.

I hid a smile. That cat could sneak around wherever he wanted. The house was riddled with concealed tunnels, and Hank knew his way through them. In the past, he'd chosen to remain hidden from her. There was a time she hadn't liked him, but now she wanted to give him a chance. Apparently, he was taking full advantage of her goodwill.

"Miss Janice," I prompted.

"Yes?" she answered absentmindedly.

"I wonder if you should get ready. The police may want to speak with you."

"What? Why on earth would they want to talk with me?"

"Well, the article does say they want to speak with all interested parties. They may consider you one since you were with him last night."

She groaned again. Her eyes fluttered closed, and she faintly waggled her bejeweled fingers to wave me away from the room.

I carried the tray with me. As I approached the door, she called to me. "Laura Lee, please send Marguerite up here."

I nodded and scurried out.

I rushed down the stairs, in the process giving the chess piece statue on the landing a pat on his head as I passed by. This beautiful knight had once saved the day and would forever be my favorite piece of artwork.

I nearly ran into Marguerite as she was leaving the kitchen.

"My word! Where's the fire?" she exclaimed, her chest puffing. Her eyes narrowed as she studied my face. "You have news, I see. Come with me."

She spun about and reentered the kitchen, dragging me along with her.

"You love my kitchen too much," Cook murmured crossly.

"Trust me, I'm not here to check up on you. Laura Lee has something to say."

I had the attention of the room, so the gossip blurted out. "Miss Janice just had one of her friends murdered!" I told them everything written in the newspaper article.

"Mr. Dee? Our neighbor?" Marguerite asked when I finished.

I nodded.

"Something evil is coming this way, mark my words," Cook mumbled as worry etched deep wrinkles by her mouth.

Marguerite didn't argue.

"Miss Janice would like you to go upstairs to her to help her in case the police show up," I said.

Marguerite nodded her head briskly. "Well, then there's nothing to it. I'm on my way."

Before she left the kitchen, she turned to me and said, "Mary dropped off Miss Janice's gala outfit this morning. They called and said it would be done by two. Please plan on picking it up sometime this afternoon."

I nodded. It made me wonder if that outfit might've been the last nice thing Mr. Dee saw before he was killed.

I started for the sink to help wash the dishes. In the process I upended a bucket. Water splashed up my pant legs, soaking me.

"Well, that's a way to make an entrance," Cook remarked. "I guess you might as well mop, too."

I grabbed a towel with a tight smile. Once again, life wanted to prove that when it rains, it does indeed pour.

CHAPTER TWO

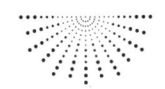

The detectives called at Thornberry manor while I was busy in the music room. Marguerite showed them to the morning room where Miss Janice waited. An hour later, when she showed them back out, her thin eyebrows were scrunched together in concern. The door had hardly shut behind the detectives when she spun toward the butler pantry, muttering something about needing to make Miss Janice her special headache tonic.

Marguerite passed the music room along the way and saw me. "You make it to the dry cleaners, yet?"

I paused from dusting the piano bench and shook my head.

"Go on now and take Mary with you." Before I could fish for any information, she marched away.

Disappointed, I jammed the dust rag back in the bag. I hated not knowing what was going on.

I found Mary in the kitchen. Her activities consisted of an enthusiastic discussion, curly hair bobbing from head movements, about all the attributes of some guy she'd met at karaoke. With the weariness of one listening to a toddler's incessant babble, Cook ignored her as she stirred a bubbling sauce with a wooden spoon. The rich scent of tomatoes hung in the air.

"You have a minute?" I interrupted. "Marguerite wants you to come with me to pick up that outfit."

Mary nodded and hopped down from the counter. After disappearing to grab her keys, we headed out.

The day was clearing now, with the clouds spreading thin to allow bits of blue to shine through.

"So what did you think about the police interviewing Miss Janice?" I asked and buckled my seatbelt.

Mary shrugged. "It's just bad luck that she was the last one to see him alive. And not only that, they shared a glass of champagne."

"They did? How do you know this?"

"I heard a bit of her statement. She was in the car that dropped him off at home. She said they toasted to show they were ending their feud. The detectives were awfully interested in their property line."

I remembered Miss Janice had mentioned he was her neighbor, but the feud was new info. "What feud?"

She shrugged. "They've been quarreling over it for years. It's really amped up recently."

Before I could ask more, she pulled into the Cream Puff bakery parking lot. I gave her a look.

"What? We have a free minute. I cleaned six bathrooms today, so I think I deserve a treat. Besides, I love their scones. And so does Marguerite."

I grinned, wondering if that's why she wanted Mary to come. We took a half dozen to go. I definitely enjoyed mine, as evidenced by my shirt covered with white crumbs. While we climbed out of the car, I tried to brush them off.

Mary laughed. "I can't take you anywhere."

"I don't know what you're laughing at me for. You have a big glob of raspberry jam on your shirt." I pointed at it without any attempt to be subtle.

Mary looked down, aghast. She swiped at it with a napkin but nothing could hide the red stain. "Of course this happens on my way into the dry cleaners. Talk about irony."

I would have laughed at the pun but then we were walking into the building. A warm puff of air that smelled both clean and floral greeted us, and a woman with a wide body and a firm bun tucked underneath a hair net scuttled out of the back room. Her name tag said Dita and the expression on her face was akin to someone who hands out poisoned apples to kids. She accepted the check stub from Mary with a grunt. I noticed Mary stand on her tiptoes to look in the back.

Before I could ask what she was doing, Dita reappeared with the garment inside a plastic bag.

Mary accepted the bag and the woman nodded before returning to the back where machines whirred and clanked.

I headed to the door but stopped when I saw Mary had paused to unzip the plastic.

"Marguerite told me to always double-check," she explained.

The bag opened to reveal a blue silk pantsuit. Impeccable creases showed down the front of the pants like twin knife blades.

"Fancy," I said.

Mary nodded and brushed her curls back impatiently. She started to zip the bag. Apparently having a second thought, she hesitated and reached into the pockets of the thin jacket.

"What are you doing?" I asked.

She kind of shrugged but her brow wrinkled as she pulled out a receipt. She turned it over and displayed the name of a gas station.

I leaned over to study it. "Okay, that's weird."

Her face was full of dismay. "It's from the gas station where Mr. Dee was found murdered."

Now it was my turn to wince. "How did that get in there?"

"I have no idea. But trust me. I'm about to find out." Her shoulders squared with determination, and she marched over to the counter and banged the little bell, showing a hot temper.

The same woman came out of the back room. Dita saw us and her eyebrows rose. "Oh, you're still here?"

"What's this?" Mary asked. She never pulled any punches and said exactly what was on her mind. Usually she managed to do it with confidence, not blundering and beating around the bush like I would.

The woman was not intimidated. "A piece of paper?"

"I see that. Why was it left in the pocket?"

"I'm not sure. Usually we check them before we dry clean." She walked over and scrutinized the jacket pocket. "It doesn't seem like it did any damage." And she nodded with relief.

"I am not asking why this was left in there for the dry cleaning," Mary said. "I want to know why it was in the pocket at all."

The woman shrugged. "How would I know why it's there? Ask your boss."

Mary's eyes narrowed suspiciously. The woman stared back and crossed her arms, which were bigger than my thighs. A large man who looked like her brother peeked through the door. He wasn't smiling either.

Mary backed down. "Thank you," she said and gathered up the outfit.

We walked to the car where the wind snatched the edge of the garment bag with a harsh rustle and threatened to tear it from her grasp. Together, we wrestled the ballooning plastic down into the trunk, and she slammed the lid down.

"What are you thinking, Mary?" I asked, pulling my sweater together to keep it safe from the grabby hands of the wind.

"I'm wondering who wore the coat."

"You don't think that woman could've worn it, do you? There's no way."

"Maybe someone else in there, then."

"Let me see the receipt again."

She handed it over, and I studied it carefully. I shook my head. "It's impossible. This is dated last night. It was before you dropped it off."

Mary's forehead was like a net that caught all the worry wrinkles. "Just between you and me, you don't think Miss Janice had anything to do with Mr. Dee's death, do you?

I laughed. "How could she? She's so tiny. The woman can't even reach the top shelf at the grocery store."

She climbed into the car, and I did the same. Hesitating, she jiggled the keys. "But you know how he's coming after her?"

"What do you mean?"

"The police were pretty persistent in their questions over the property line."

I rolled my eyes. Rich people. Why would they fight over fifteen feet of either side of the property line? Why couldn't they just be happy? "I thought you said they shared champagne to acknowledge a truce."

"What if that's not true?"

"You think she lied?"

Mary lifted a thin shoulder. "Not really. However, I don't know if you knew this, but Miss Janice was home late last night. And she seemed quite a bit shook up."

I couldn't see it. "Don't be ridiculous."

"Maybe we need to go look at that fifteen feet to see what all the interest was about," Mary said, finally starting the car. We pulled out onto the road.

"That might be a good idea. But with this receipt, I think we need to involve the book club."

After we returned to the house, Mary handed the outfit and bag of scones to Marguerite.

"Everything okay?" Marguerite asked. That woman could discern if a blue-bottle fly was having a bad day.

"Yeah," Mary said noncommittally. I think she wanted to hold off answering any questions from Marguerite. Like she had a chance of that working.

"What's going on?" Marguerite asked smartly.

"We need a meeting later," Mary whispered. "A very private one."

Marguerite's eyes widened, but she gave a brisk nod.

"The usual time, then. I'll spread the word," she said. "Now go help get that dinner prepared. Plumbers just left, thank heavens for small things." With that, Marguerite spun on her heels to stride up the stairwell with the suspicious outfit slung over her arm.

CHAPTER THREE

In the past, our book club meetings had disintegrated into a bunch of random chitchat, none of which circled around books. Tonight was no exception. One notable difference was that no one showed up late.

The girls lounged in their favorite spots while candles bathed the room in flickering light. Two plates of my favorite cookies sat on the table, chocolate chip and spicy oatmeal raisin. Cook relaxed on her beloved easy chair, her striped socked feet poking out onto the ottoman.

"All right, let's get this show on the road," Cook said. "Are we even going to pretend to talk about the book?"

"I can't. After all I haven't even had a chance to get into A Christmas Carol," Jessie muttered. This was not new for her. "I thought we had another whole week to go."

"That's what you get for procrastinating," Lucy said.

Jessie shot her a look. "It's not my fault that I have so many chores."

Cook scoffed. "Could it be because you're on your cell phone all day, mooning over your newest boy toy."

Everyone laughed, even Jessie.

Marguerite walked to the front and heavily leaned against the desk. Her gaze swept around the room. "I'm sure we've all heard the rather upsetting news regarding our Miss Janice."

The room quieted down, with some girls nodding. Most watched her like cows waiting for the farmer to feed them. They were hungry for the juicy scoop.

"Well, what's the news?" Cook asked, wiggling her toes. "Don't be keeping us in suspense."

"Today, when Mary and Laura Lee arrived at the dry cleaners to pick up Miss Janice's outfit from the gala, they found something in the pocket."

Immediately the ladies's heads swiveled in my direction. I didn't like the expressions several of them wore. Like they were hurt I'd kept something from them.

I swallowed hard.

Marguerite grabbed the room's attention again with a clap of her hands. She held out the offending receipt. "This was found in the pocket of Miss Janice's gala outfit the other night. It's for a gas station."

Of course, everyone gasped.

"How did it get in her pocket?" Janet asked.

"If we knew that, it wouldn't be a mystery, now would it?" Marguerite answered, dryly.

Janet cleared her throat. "I have something to say." Her color reminded me of cottage cheese, and I hope she felt okay. When she saw she had our attention, she reached into a paper bag and pulled out a handkerchief. It was covered in red-brown, the color of dried blood.

"Where did you find that?" Mary demanded, sitting forward.

Janet flipped her thin blonde braid off her shoulder. She managed to appear even paler. "Stuffed behind the vase in the foyer."

My eyebrows raised. That definitely led in a concerning direction.

Janet continued, "Last night Miss Janice came home very flustered. I found her wandering in the foyer and asked if she needed help. She told me no and went to her room. It was after that I went over to the vase and found this."

Everyone spoke at once. Someone else asked, "Do we take the handkerchief to the police?"

"Maybe we should ask Miss Janice about it," Lucy said. I noticed the lisp.

"And give her a heart-attack? We already know she knew nothing about the murder." Marguerite crossed her arms.

"I wonder what the police had to say when they were here?" Janet asked.

"Just the usual questions about the gala." Mary looked queasy. "And something about the property line fight."

Everyone looked at Mary.

She shrugged. "What? The wainscoting was extra dusty in the hallway outside her bedroom."

"Just outside her door? I bet the wood is all shiny-like now." Cook grinned and gave her a thumbs up.

"Cook, that's abhorrent behavior. We don't eavesdrop in this house." Marguerite stared down her nose.

Cook shot a sarcastic eye roll to the ceiling. "Everyone step away from Marguerite."

"What on earth are you saying?" Marguerite demanded.

"I'm warning everyone about the lightning that's sure to strike you."

Marguerite clearly wasn't impressed, and there was a stare-down between the two ladies that lasted several silent seconds. I think we were all invested. Who would speak first?

Apparently, Marguerite. With a slow blink and nostrils flaring from a weary sigh, she returned her attention to the room. "For now, I say we keep this to ourselves. If anyone hears anything more," she stared hard at Mary, "Please let us know right away. We all know Miss Janice has no one but us to protect her."

Cook snorted. "That woman could scare a dinosaur."

"You're a dinosaur," Marguerite popped back. She smiled gently at us as if to prove she was the rational one. "We're all she has. Especially after... you know who."

We nodded. Miss Janice's last love affair had ended in a disaster. It seemed the group relaxed enough to settle down to discuss the book and get to some real snacking. Of course, that's when thundering footsteps and a knock on the secret door interrupted it all.

CHAPTER FOUR

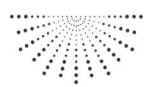

"*S*orry to barge in." Butler stood in the hidden bookcase doorway, nervously wringing his long thin fingers.

"Butler, this is supposed to be a secret meeting." Marguerite sank down into her chair, clearly exasperated by the whole thing.

"I understand."

"It's our secret room. You're ruining that." She waved a limp hand at him.

"I'm sorry. Something came for Miss Janice."

"And what's that?"

He held out a notebook paper, and I noticed it was shaking. Marguerite stared at it, unimpressed. He realized he held it backward and clumsily turned it around.

In red ink, it said, *I know what you did. You won't get away with it.*

I gasped, while Mary cursed and Lucy squealed. The ripple of outrage proceeded through the room.

The paper continued to tremble as if it were indignant as well. "I found it on the front porch under a rock. I heard a knock but no one was there."

"Do we call the police?" Jessie asked.

"Maybe that's best," Butler answered.

"What? I say not! I'm sure this will turn into some type of extortion, but right now the police will most likely turn their heads even more her way. Let's keep our eyes open and see if anything else happens. This could just be a prank from one of the local kids," Cook said.

I didn't say anything, but I did wonder how a kid would get past the gate. Then again, anything was possible.

"Why do they think Miss Janice had a motive to do this?" I asked.

"The property line of course. Everyone's talking about how odd it was he took a ride in her car," Jessie said, nodding her head adamantly.

Again, the property line. It seemed like such an easy problem to solve. "What about the surveyors?"

"They've had several surveyors out and they've all come to the same conclusion. I'm not sure why, but it has to do with both Mr. Dee and Miss Janice ancestors who first settled here, before the land was properly marked."

"I don't get it. Even still, who cares? They both have a massive amount of property."

"The big deal is that there's a little village down there," Cook said, sitting back with another cookie. She broke it in two and popped the half into her mouth.

"Really?" I sat up, surprised.

"Actually it's just a set of two houses and a small church built around the time this town started," she mumbled around the crumbs.

"Who built it?"

"The Thornberry ancestors."

I laughed. "That seems like the answer to the problem right there."

"It would seem that way, except Mr. Dee said it was on his property."

"I see." I really didn't but I said it anyway. "Still that doesn't seem like a motive for murder."

This time Janet answered. "This all started after the elementary school's historical tour there several years ago. It was quite the adventure."

"What happened?" Lucy asked.

"A school teacher led her fifth grade class through one building. It's a rather neat area since there are some remaining untouched tools and the church still has the original bell," Janet explained. She was one of those people who was addicted to facts.

"Okay," I said, still waiting for the big reveal.

"So there was this brother and a sister in the class. As often happens, the two engaged in a huge fight with each other. The teacher tried to separate them. The girl was so mad she went to go find her mother, who was one of the voluntary teacher aids for the trip. The boy was afraid he would get in trouble so he ran and hid."

Several of the women nodded, familiar with the story.

"Well, then the whole hullabaloo was that no one could find the boy. They searched and searched. And finally they corralled all the kids on the bus and the police were called. There was a fear he had fallen down a well."

"Oh, no," I said.

"They found the old well with the cover off. But the search showed that nobody was inside. So, they brought in a helicopter and a team to spread out over the grass. It was horrendous. Just when everything seemed to be at the worst, the boy came out of a closet."

"What? They didn't search the closet?" I was thunderstruck.

"I swear after this place, I wonder if it had a false wall. The kid came out and said that he had found a bunch of treasure."

"Treasure!" I yelled. "What kind of treasure?"

"No one knows. They searched the closet and couldn't find a way in or out. They chocked it all up to the kid going in there and falling asleep."

"Really? That's ridiculous. Who sleeps when there's a crowd of people calling your name?" I asked.

She shrugged. "They didn't see anything. Still you can imagine the wild fires those rumors caused."

Butler cleared his throat.

Marguerite rose to her feet and took the paper. She stared down at it. "Thank you, Butler. You are ever diligent."

"I'll be looking into installing one of those do-hickey cameras. I will catch them next time." He left and the false bookshelf door shuddered into place.

Mary nudged my shoulder. "You know what this means, don't you?"

I nodded.

"What does it mean?" Lucy demanded, poking her face closer.

"Why, we need to go down there and check it out for ourselves."

"We?" Lucy asked.

"Sure. Whoever wants to come along."

"Tomorrow at lunch. It's a plan." I said before Marguerite called the meeting to end like a teacher releasing a school class.

* * *

THE NEXT DAY MARY, Lucy, and I gathered in the backyard. No one else wanted to go, with Jessie insisting we were bananas because the walk was too far.

Her comment worried me. Still, we all wore our sneakers with the exception of Mary, who had on pink hiking boots. The sun shone warm and bright, and my heart filled with cheer to be out on this beautiful summer day.

"Ready, ladies?" I asked.

We walked to the far side of the great lawn and through the many flower gardens. A tiny dot in the distance eventually came into focus as Stephen on the lawnmower. I waved and he waved back. He paused the mower and gave us a curious look. No surprise there. I'm sure we were all a funny sight, what with Lucy's hat on sideways, Mary's oversized sunglasses, and a scarf swathed over her head like some old-time movie star.

We walked past the manicured hedges, the boxwood, the red-berried holly, and the flowering quince, with the birds chirping and butterflies lazily fluttering ahead, and then we entered the apple orchard. The sun dappled the ground in lemon splotches through the overhead leaves.

"How much further?" I asked, remembering Jessie's warning.

"Girl, you're the one that wanted to come here. She owns over two hundred acres, you know," Lucy said.

"Terrific," I said as my internal temperature started to rise under the summer sun.

We meandered through a field of wild grass that buzzed with clouds of little bugs. I covered my face with my shirt. Trust me to be the one to breathe them in and choke on the swarm. I could just see my poor mom trying to write that obituary. I was no country girl. I couldn't understand how no one else cared about the insects, other than Lucy casually swiping in front of her face. I had to wipe my face as well, but mine came from sweat that seemed to be perfume, attracting the pests.

Something in the grass ahead of us jumped. A little brown bunny watched us with bright alert eyes, his nose twitching. Sweat tickled along my spine, and I felt great remorse at coming all this way during the hottest part of the day. I would've regretted my pants as well except for all the bugs in the grass.

We approached a huge tree and a thick line of blackberries. After a moment, I saw that the berry bushes fenced in two buildings. In the background rose the mountain peak of the famous Goat Mountain. This mountain could be seen from nearly every point of our town but was especially breathtaking from here.

We entered what might have been the front yard. The dry, flat area now bristled with weeds and small saplings.

"That's the work office." Mary pointed to a gray building. The sun had bleached the wood into a pale gray, and the building stairs sank like a wooden hammock.

"The teacher brought the kids through that?" I asked, doubtfully.

Mary shook her head. "No. That's where the boy said he'd ended up underground. The teacher took them through the church over there." She pointed to a small stone building where indeed I could see a steeple rising with the bell in the tower.

Just then, I heard a male voice booming from the other direction. And even worse, red lights flashed, practically spelling out danger.

CHAPTER FIVE

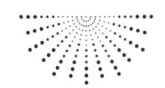

The police were here. Great. Now we had to come up with an explanation for why we were here, and fast. I spotted yellow tape—too late to warn us now—as it fluttered in the wind around the church's porch posts.

One of the officers nudged his buddy, and they both watched us, their eyes hidden behind dark sunglasses. His buddy said something and the first guy dipped his head and strode over.

"Can I help you?" he asked.

My brain went blank leaving me completely at a loss for words. All I could think about was the threatening note from last night. "Don't make Miss Janice look even more guilty," my inner voice warned. Lucy gave a nervous giggle and hid behind me.

Once again, Mary took one for the team. She smiled, her fresh face and curls appearing simultaneously innocent and charming. "We recently heard about the children's field trip that took place here and wanted to check out the historical landmark ourselves."

"There's an investigation going on right now." The statement was as powerful as a closing door.

My tongue finally loosened from the roof of my mouth. "Is it a crime scene?"

"We received an anonymous tip we're checking out."

"Okay. We didn't know. We'll get out of your hair," Mary said. He nodded, so all us girls turned around and started back in the direction of the manor.

I heard a cough and shot a glance over my shoulder. From across the property line I saw someone walking away, as well. Someone in a red plaid sports jacket.

"Who's that guy in the jacket?" I asked, gesturing behind us.

Mary looked. "Mikey Dee. Mr. Dee's son."

"Weird he's also here at the exact time the police are."

She grimly smiled. "Makes you kind of wonder who the anonymous source really was."

"Maybe the same person who left the note last night?"

She watched him go, her eyebrows arched in anger. "He'll be in a world of trouble if I find out it was him."

We only had time for a quick lunch when we got back. Of course, Cook wanted to hear all about our adventure.

I gave her the disappointingly brief details, punctuated with lots of adjectives to describe the word hot, as I snagged a cookie from the cooling rack.

She huffed when she learned Mikey had been there. "What's that boy up to, I wonder?"

"Boy? He looked older than me," Lucy said, digging into the peanut butter with a spoon.

Cook's eyes grew in horror as Lucy scooped up a blob. "What's wrong with you? Who does that?"

"I like it." Lucy shrugged, licking the spoon.

"Anyway," I said. "I think we need some more history on this property. For instance, why are the buildings there?"

Cook reluctantly dragged her attention away. "Well, that's easy, isn't it? We have to have a book talking all about it, I'm sure."

"Really?"

"You betcha. Family history and all that. We come from strong stock."

I loved how she included herself in the Thornberry family history, but then again she'd been working for the family since she was a teenager. Cook glanced around the kitchen, where the roast sat in the oven and the French bread rested with a towel over it on the counter. "We've got some time now. Let's go quick and take a peek."

Her mind made up, she headed out, with us following behind. I always felt bad entering Marguerite's room and tried to do it as quietly as possible. Even tip-toeing at times, as though I were entering a hospital room.

Cook, however, had other intentions and banged the door open as she barged through the doorway.

I swear Marguerite has a sixth sense that was downright spooky at times. As if the door had been armed with an alarm, Marguerite showed up mere minutes later. "What on earth are you doing here?" she snapped.

"We're trying to save Miss Janice," Cook returned fire as she shuffled with the contraption to open the secret door.

"And how does my room pertain to this great salvation plan?"

"These girls have a theory about the back forty. I'm sure we have a book on it." She wiggled the shelf and the secret door opened.

Marguerite watched, arms crossed, as Cook made her way to the bookshelves.

"Let me see…." Cook rubbed her lower back in soothing circles as the finger on her other hand ran along the spines. She paused now and again to read a title. "Ah! Here it is." She gave a pleased, throaty chuckle and pulled out a thin hardcover. "Look."

She held the book out like it was the winning pie at a country fair. I tried to read the title, but she'd already pulled it back and began to scan the table of contents. After a moment, she thumbed through the pages, stopping with a smug grin. She pointed the book back in our direction again.

The page displayed a sepia picture of trees. It could have been anywhere until I spotted the craggy top of Goat Mountain in the background.

However, instead of a house, there were several canvas tents. The next picture showed a group of people standing before the white church. Their faces were stern and proud. Several had handkerchiefs over their faces. It was not hard to believe there could be a gold mine underneath.

Cook began to read. "The first settlers were…" She began coughing, her face turning red.

Marguerite rolled her eyes. "Give me that." She snatched the book away. Lifting her chin, she reached into her shirt front and fished out a pair of glasses dangling from a chain. She studied the page with a wise look. Her eyebrows raised like she was a teacher about to give an important class lesson.

In the meantime, Cook sank into her favorite seat. I perched on the edge of the bench next to her.

"I did that on purpose," she whispered to me with a grin. "I've always hated reading out loud." With a satisfied air, she plucked a cookie from her apron pocket and took a bite.

Marguerite began, "Settlers came to this wonderful land. Two families rose above the rest of the homesteaders, the Thornberrys and the Blackstones. Together, they built a church. It was a place where all were welcome to worship God. Later, one of the young men found a cavern hidden behind a large rock. It led to a cave far below. They climbed down and it is believed they discovered gold. Their excitement restored them, and they believed the Lord rewarded them for putting God first by bringing them this treasure. They built the house over it after they excavated what they could. In later years, the building was turned into a schoolhouse. The buildings were saved by the owner for posterity."

When she finished, she shut the book, and took off her glasses with a solemn air.

"Well, that was disappointing," Lucy announced.

"How on earth?" Marguerite scolded. "That's the Thornberry legacy."

"What? It didn't tell us anything. We're in the same spot we were to begin with. Seriously. We don't even know if there was a gold mine. Why can't they just say who the land belongs to?"

That certainly would have made things easier.

"We know who the property belongs to. The. Thornberrys." With full stops, Marguerite sniffed as if to dare someone to argue with her.

"Then why did Mr. Dee think he had a leg to stand on?" I asked.

"He didn't. He just wanted to muddy the waters so he could get the gold," scoffed Mary.

"Let's bring up the second problem. What are we going to do with Miss Janice being threatened?"

"We ignore it," Mary said.

"Ignore it. With the neighbor next door murdered," huffed Cook. She adjusted her pink glitter headband.

Marguerite noticed the movement. "Just how many of those do you have, anyway?"

"Why?" snapped Cook.

"Because you're always wearing it."

"I like pink. I like headbands. So sue me," Cook responded.

Marguerite pursed her lips like she had a good comeback when Cook continued. "Besides, this is about Miss Janice's life, or have you forgotten?"

"Of course not!"

"Maybe you can't multi-task any more," Cook said. "Can't keep focused. It can be an issue."

"An issue of what?" Marguerite's feathers were ruffled.

"Some say of age," said Cook, shrugging.

"Age? I'll have you know you're older than me!"

"Hardly!"

We watched this like a terrifying tennis match. None of us were brave enough to get involved.

"Ladies!" Mary said.

I guess one of us was brave enough.

The two women turned to her. "Miss Janice and the threat. It's not just her, you know. If someone tries to follow through with it, all of us are in danger. How can we track down who left the note?"

At that moment, Marguerite's phone rang. "Hello?" she answered. She stiffened immediately. "I'm sorry, ma'am. I'm on my way." Then she glanced at Mary. "I'll send them up right now." She hung up.

"What?" Lucy asked.

"That was Miss Janice. The police are here in the foyer. They want to discuss the receipt in the pocket. Apparently, the dry cleaners called them."

CHAPTER SIX

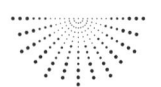

My heart dropped when I came downstairs and saw the same two officers from the church earlier standing in the entryway. No number of pats on the lucky chess statue would get me out of this.

Unfortunately, they recognized us as well, as acknowledged with lifted eyebrows. "You two are in the mix of things again?" said the one who'd addressed us at the church.

"It's one of those weird coincidences," Mary said with her quick grin.

"Coincidence for what?" he shot back.

His question stopped her speedy wit.

"Your name?"

Mary gave it. He brought out a notebook. "I heard you found something in the pocket of an outfit that came from here. We have a witness at the dry cleaners who saw it in your hand."

We both nodded.

"Where is the item now?"

Mary's expression was both innocent and honest. "I threw it away after I showed the clerk. She assured me the fabric had not been damaged by it. That's all I was worried about."

"You don't have it?" he asked again.

"Why would I keep it? It was just a scrap piece of paper."

"We were told it was a receipt."

Mary shrugged. "I wouldn't know."

"You didn't unfold it to see?"

My skin felt prickly in anticipation at how Mary would answer that question.

"I thought it was some receipt to the store or something. Once I saw it wasn't a handwritten note, I tossed it, since it was of no importance."

"You can't remember anything else?"

She shook her head, with me imitating like her shadow.

The officer dismissed us with a stern request to contact them if we should remember anything.

We left and relief shot through me in a rush. I had to force myself not to run. We immediately headed for the butler's pantry. Mary slammed the door behind us and leaned against it with a deep exhale.

I whispered to Mary, "How did the dry cleaner know it was a receipt? Or what it said? You never gave it to her."

She brushed one of her flyaways from her face. "I know. That's why I responded the way I did. As soon as he said that I realized they must have set Miss Janice up."

Janet came in with a glass decanter. "Well, that was something, now wasn't it?"

Mary rummaged through a drawer for white gloves and handed me a pair. We began to polish the crystal for dinner service. My senses were on fire as I listened for the front door to signal that the police had left.

"I did what I had to do. Now we need to find out why the dry cleaners wanted to set up Miss Janice. Maybe go back for a little visit? Either of you have anything that can be dry cleaned?" Mary asked.

I shook my head, suddenly very apprehensive.

"I might have something," Janet said quietly, twirling her thin blonde braid around her finger.

"You do?"

"A sweater."

"Fantastic. Tomorrow, we're going to do some reconnaissance."

"In other words, some poking around," Janet said.

"Another lunch date then."

We all grinned.

* * *

Late afternoon on the next day found the three of us squashed in Mary's tiny car with Janet's sweater in her hand. She waved it like a victory flag, insisting she was sure we'd find some answers.

After a quick squabble discussing who would be best to take it into the dry cleaners, we all ended up inside.

The big, burly guy was at the counter this time, the one who'd peered at us through the door when we'd been there earlier.

"Hi, there," Mary said. Her eyebrows flicked up hopeful-like. "I'm looking for the gal who helped us earlier. Name was Dita?"

"She doesn't work here anymore," he answered gruffly, his thick eyebrows furrowing low over his eyes.

"How about this young guy, Dylan? I saw him when I dropped off a pantsuit."

"He's gone too." He accepted the sweater and gave Janet a ticket.

Mary's optimistic expression fizzled when the man took the sweater through the swinging doors without another word. He never reappeared.

The second hand on the clock on the wall ticked, and the whole moment felt very anticlimactic. We slowly returned outside like scolded puppies.

Mary leaned against the hood while we spread out in front of her. It seemed all of us were reluctant to get back in the car.

"Where now, brown cow?" Mary finally asked.

"What were you expecting?" I asked.

"I thought maybe we'd see the woman again and at least get to ask a question. How was I to know this job was on a lazy Susan rotation?"

A green sign across the street grabbed my attention. I squinted to read it. "What about the library? Maybe we'll find something new there about the Thornberry estate."

Even though Mary wanted to drive, Janet and I convinced her to walk. The bright sunshine might have been intimidating on some days, but after being stuck in the house all day, it was a gorgeous escape, as long as we weren't on a gnat-filled trek through the Thornberry property.

Historic buildings made this part of town notable, all brick and massive, with unique cornices and window treatments. The library was no exception. The brass plaque on the front stated it was the library, but when we walked up the stairs, a hand-painted sign said, **Twice Again**.

"What the heck?" Mary asked. She yanked open the door.

It was definitely not a library. Instead of books and a quiet hush, what we encountered was bangle music, chaotic shelves and tables lined with do-dads, and the eclectic colors of vintage clothing and scarves.

The lady in charge of the store approached us, just as colorful as the shop's wares. Her giant skirt patterned with giant red poppies wafted around her as if moved by a spring breeze. A lemon yellow shirt and a red scarf completed the ensemble, while chandelier earrings swung from very stretched out earlobes that spoke of a history of such bedazzled abuse. She wore not one speck of makeup but her eyes were bright and her cheeks pink. "Welcome. My name is Harmony."

The entire thrift store practically begged to be explored. Of course, we had to concede to the desire.

"So, you've just moved in here?" Mary asked, examining a knickknack from one table.

"Yes, that's right. Just last year. I have such great memories of coming to the library as a kid. When it popped up for rent I had to grab it. It was a dream come true." Harmony gave a sleepy, relaxed smile.

Mary and I looked at each other. Someone at our fingertips with real background experience here. "So you know a lot about the history of the town?" I asked.

"Of course. It's steeped in fascinating stories. But who knows exactly what is true." She made spooky fingers.

"We're interested in the bit about the Thornberrys and Mr. Dee." Mary picked up a miniature glass horse, examined it, and set it back down.

Harmony nodded with her eyes half-closed, giving her a wise-owl expression. "I see. It's been all over the news."

"His death?"

"And the gold."

"So, who do you think owns the land?" I asked.

"Why, Mr. Dee, of course." She sounded shocked I'd even question the ownership.

"How is that?" Mary asked, a little hotly. She really was a ride-or-die friend, even for the Thornberrys.

"Well, they were here longer than the Thornberrys. They went by the Blackstones back then."

My eyes flew open. I'd never even considered there had been a name change. This made things much more complicated.

"Do you know where we can find any information about them?" I asked.

"You had the right idea about the library. They've relocated two streets over."

We spent another ten minutes meandering about the store and nearly escaped with our wallets unscathed. However Mary did find a pair of earrings. As we walked back to the car, Janet searched for the directions to the library on the phone. Unfortunately she then squashed our optimism when she announced it was closed. Discouraged, we started back home. Along the way, we stopped at a red light by the dry cleaners once again.

I was daydreaming out the window when Janet squealed, "Oh, my gosh! Do you see what I see? Right there!"

I turned to where she pointed.

"Can you believe that? Look at that guy, seriously! What a creeper!" Mary scowled, the motion making her hair appear to quiver in indignation.

Usually it was difficult to pick a random person out of a crowd. Normally, people kept their heads down, somewhat distracted with their phone or window shopping. Very rarely did people look at other people as they walked.

And that's what this guy was doing. First he glanced over his shoulder in the most suspicious way, and scanned the crowd. Apparently he didn't find what he was searching for because he pulled his hat further down his forehead.

One thing that stood out to me was his plaid jacket. It was the same jacket I saw at the property line.

"Mikey!" Mary gave a little whistle.

"He's skulking, isn't he?" Janet said.

Mary snorted. "Skulking? Is that your word of the day?"

"What's he doing now?" I redirected her attention.

"He's talking to that pregnant lady. And she's wearing the dry cleaner's uniform."

"Who is she?" Mary asked. The car behind us beeped to let us know the light was green.

"Maybe a new employee?" I searched on my phone for the dry cleaners. Again, I was disappointed. They only had a simple advertising page with no list of employees.

I glanced out the back window as we drove away. The two seemed awfully friendly. Then I saw them both look in our direction. He smiled and nodded, making me duck my head.

Who was that woman to Mikey? Was that his child? And most import of all, had he asked her to slip the gas station receipt into Miss Janice's pocket?

CHAPTER SEVEN

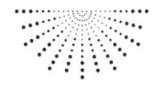

That evening found me trapped in a hot laundry room, hauling sheets out of the dryer with two more loads waiting their turn through the machines. It felt like I was moving underwater, so sweaty and exhausted all I could think about was my bed and pulling the covers over my head. I wanted to forget about everything else. Threatening notes, dead bodies, dry cleaner receipts.

The door banged open, scaring me. I jumped to see Lucy practically dance through the doorway in her excitement.

"What's going on?" I asked.

"I've been looking everywhere for you," she said in a sing-song.

Her energy was all aflutter with her news. Feeling flattered, I shook out a warm towel. "I'm all ears."

"So, my boyfriend Larry just called me. I'm totally shocked," she lisped the last few words.

"Really? What did he say?"

I thought the next words would be something about a marriage proposal. Instead, she blurted out, "He bartended at the hotel where the gala was held last week!"

"Wow! Did he see Mr. Dee?"

She nodded. "And Miss Janice. But neither really caught his attention other than their drinks. He has a photographic memory and can retain anything. It's so annoying to argue with him." She made a face.

I would hear about her domestic troubles later. Right now I wanted the goods. "And?"

"He said later Mr. Dee returned with another man. The two had a conversation that's bothered him ever since Mr. Dee's death."

"What was it?"

"It centered around Mr. Dee's son. I guess they're estranged."

"Seriously?"

"That's what Larry heard."

I frowned. "Maybe he misunderstood. Maybe it was engaged."

Lucy shrugged. "Like I said, Larry has a great memory. He can make a drink after learning about it once."

I didn't want to insinuate I doubted her. "Of course. Now does he know if the conversation was about Mikey? Or did Mr. Dee have more than one son?"

"I'm not sure. Interesting though since I've always heard family comes first as a murder suspect. I wonder what the estrangement was all about. Do you think it could involve something that made Mikey want revenge?"

I shook out a pillow case. "I just find it hard to believe the police would overlook such an obvious suspect. Still, the idea that his son is behind this makes me sick. You never know what the world is coming to. It's evil sometimes."

"Evil world?" Mary had walked by the laundry room and reversed her steps to peer in. "What am I missing?"

"We were talking about Lucy's boyfriend."

"Who do I need to kill?" Mary calmly asked, her hand flexing.

I laughed. "No one."

"He's a good guy," Lucy stammered.

"Okay, good. That's all I need to hear. He was about to experience me hopping on his head like a spider monkey. I'd take him down."

Now we both laughed. The visual was hilarious. Lucy filled her in on the overheard conversation at the bar.

Before we could get into it any deeper, Marguerite came bustling by like a plump hen. She sent Mary to turn down Miss Janice's room. Lucy scuttled away and I was left, once again, to stew in my thoughts in the humid room.

That night, when I climbed into bed, first scooting Hank over to make room for my feet, fear struck me. What if Mikey knew we were searching into him? When we'd seen him today, he sure appeared like he recognized us. Was he really in control of this game, even two steps ahead, while we were simply trying to play catch up?

CHAPTER EIGHT

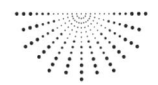

I woke up the next morning to a beautiful sunrise. The light of the sun licked the edges of the leaves on the tree outside my window with pink light. I didn't care. A specific thought took up all the space in my mind. A single word, really.

Coffee. I dressed and struggled down the stairs, feeling more zombie-like than human. Still, I couldn't resist patting the knight chess statue before staggering into the kitchen.

The general morning crew had already gathered, mostly grouped around the table, with Cook at the oven. I snagged a mug from the cupboard, poured some coffee, then brought it to the table.

Cook shuffled over in fluffy pink slippers with a tall stack of pancakes on a plate. Those fat slippers made me smile. I grabbed a pancake and leaned across the table for the syrup.

"Where did you get those?" I asked.

"These old things? They were a gift." Despite her downplaying, I noticed her eyes took on a shiny look.

Marguerite snorted. "You didn't have those last week. Don't tell me you have Danny-boy back in your life."

Cook sliced a grapefruit in half and set it on a plate. Her lips pressed into two indignant lines instead of answering.

Marguerite groaned and slapped her forehead. "Oh no. You are, aren't you? You're talking with Danny-boy again? Didn't you learn your lesson the last time he got out of jail?"

"I'll have you know that this time is going to be different," Cook said indignantly. "And I am not discussing any of this with you."

Mary and Lucy watched the whole exchange with the peaked interest of two cats staring at a butterfly.

"Guess who we saw at the dry cleaners' yesterday," I said to change the subject. "Mikey." I shoved a bite of delicious goodness in my mouth and chewed while getting out my phone to search for some info about the neighbor's son.

"Probably preparing his suit for the funeral," Marguerite mused. She dipped her teabag in the water a few times.

"Weird," I accidentally murmured, while reading what the search engine brought up.

"What did you find?" Mary asked. Her thick hair was tied back in a wild ponytail.

"Mr. Dee's name popped up on the local police page. Get this, he called in a stolen vehicle."

"His Lincoln?"

"Yes, that's right."

Marguerite shook her head, her steel-colored curls wobbling. "Maybe that's why he needed a ride with Miss Janice. Mr. Dee hasn't been doing well. I wonder if he got confused."

"He doesn't have a chauffeur?"

She sipped her tea. "I don't think he's had a driver for some time. I think that the estate has been run down a little bit."

"Where did the money go, do you think?" Lucy asked.

"We've heard rumors." Cook nodded sagely.

"Yeah, probably through Danny-boy," Marguerite shot back.

"Hey, Danny-boy might have problems, but he's a good man and might be able to help us, so there."

"Wait, there's more." I said, still reading. "It looks like last year Mikey got arrested for check fraud."

"That makes sense to me. He spends an awful lot of time at one of those gambling places."

"You mean Las Vegas?"

"Guys like him don't go to public places like Las Vegas. They have their own special gambling rooms," Mary said.

I scrolled through the news some more. "I wonder if Mr. Dee's car was ever found. Do you think the police are looking into it?"

"Well, my cousin might know," Janet said. "I could bug him and find out."

"That's a great idea," I said. Mary nodded as she buttered a blueberry muffin. I looked at the muffin and wanted a bite. But how many carbs could be excused for breakfast?

Janet sent a text. "I'll let you know what he says."

I finished breakfast and took my plate to the sink. Jessie was already there with a basin full of soap bubbles.

"Just stick it in there," she said.

"Thanks."

Then I grabbed the tray Cook finished and brought it up to Miss Janice along with the single fresh flower.

Once in her room, I set the tray down on her table and walked over to the curtains. I pulled them wide just the way she liked, and then set to straightening her room a tiny bit.

"Laura Lee, can you please crack the window? I wanted to feel the fresh breeze," Miss Janice called from the bed.

"Sure thing."

Easier said than done. I struggled to open the window. Like all of this entire house it was old and cranky and stuck in its ways. I pushed and finally succeeded in raising the wooden casement three inches.

"That's nice. It looks like a beautiful morning," she said. "And can you please draw me a bath? I have a luncheon this afternoon. Pull my canary suit as well."

"Yes, Miss Janice," I said. I entered her massive, white marble bathroom and turned on the bathwater in her claw tub. Then I went into her closet for her yellow business suit. Finding it, I placed it on the dressing table.

"See if you can find a hat that goes with it," her wavering voice called from the bed.

I stared at the shelves. That was something more of a search. All the hats were kept in boxes.

"I believe it's in the pink one. On the highest shelf," she called.

Finally I spied it. I pulled the ladder over and climbed up, and then brought it over to the dressing bench. Then, I found the matching shoes I knew she'd ask for before I put the ladder away. Her shoes were very sensible.

I finished off her bath with lavender salts and returned to her bedside.

She thanked me. "You can collect the tray in an hour." She opened up the newspaper.

Sixty minutes later on the dot, I returned upstairs. The mood was completely different. Miss Janice had not moved from the bed. Even more dreadful, she looked like she had shrunken to half her size.

Although the room temperature was warm, she whispered, "Please shut the window. I'm freezing."

"Miss Janice, are you all right?" I asked.

She stared at me with a haunted look as though she had seen a ghost. Then she shook her head. "No, no. I'm not all right."

"What on earth's the matter," I asked, very concerned. Especially when I saw she hadn't even taken one bite of her toast.

"Just close the window, like I asked."

I hurried to the window to tug it down. It proved to be just as stubborn as going up, and I wrestled with it for a moment before I succeeded.

"Latch it, please," she said in a quiet voice.

I locked it tight and then walked over to the bedside. "What's the matter, Miss Janice?"

She seemed reluctant to tell me and instead just stared at me with eyes almost childlike now in their fright. Finally, she pointed to the newspaper.

I glanced down to see what it was she had read, expecting some horrid headline stating a tragedy. Was it another friend?

Instead, it was the classifieds. Confused I looked at her again. This time, her familiar expression of frustration made the wrinkles at her eyes whisk out.

"Read it," she demanded, stabbed the paper hard enough to leave a dent.

"I'm not sure—"

"Look at the Personals," she said.

I scanned the column, my eyes jumping over the usual brunettes who like long walks that made up the ads. Then my eye stopped because the next one, in capital letters, read, "We Know What You Did, Janice T."

My mouth dropped open, and I stared at her. I couldn't imagine her thoughts at reading that there.

She gazed back plaintively, her eyes wide. "I was just looking. I know it's silly at my age but sometimes you can find a companion that way. I'm not into all the Tweet Box and other internet dating things. This is all I have."

"Of course." My heart squeezed. I knew she desired a companion, somebody just to share the day-to-day conversation with. I would never find fault in her searching like that. "I understand," I said. "This is horrible. Who would write this?"

She shook her head and pulled her wrap tighter around herself. "I have no idea."

I didn't know what to say. I realized her bath must be ice cold by now. "Would you like me to draw you a new bath?"

She shook her head. "No, no. I can't go to that luncheon now."

"Why not?" I asked.

"Because the whole world will have probably read this," she snapped. And then her voice softened. "Besides, I'm scared now." She glanced around the room. "These walls at least will keep me safe."

CHAPTER NINE

Of course I told Mary what happened, who told Lucy, who told Janet, who told Jessie, who told Cook, and then Marguerite, who probably told Butler. Butler didn't really speak to us—he didn't talk much at all—but I assumed he knew by the especially glowering glare he gave the newspaper as he threw it out.

News traveled fast at the manor. I think we were all devastated that our Miss Janice had been targeted again. But by who? How could we find out?

I grabbed my cleaning caddy and headed for the study. This was my favorite room in the house, all cozy with its deep brown tapestry rug, a flower pattern running through it with thick red thread. Not to mention all the secret reading nooks.

However, I was alone in my appreciation of the study. Mary said it reminded her of a stuffy old classroom.

After a splash of lemon oil, I ran the dust rag along the top rail of the wainscoting. The bottom panel popped open and out sauntered Hank with his tail like a flagpole.

"Hi buddy," I said. He brritted at me, melting my resistance, so I sank to the floor for a cuddle. He stretched his legs to make a show of delaying, and then came over and climbed in my lap. He didn't try to situate himself and instead stood with all of his great weight on two itty-bitty feet on my thigh.

"Good grief, boy. Can you at least curl up a little?" I gave him a good long snuggle. I swear he must have known I needed some comfort, because he blinked those olive green eyes at me and smiled in his cat way before giving me a little purr.

I loved his purr. Extremely rare, it made me feel like a rock star when I could get him to do it. After a minute, I reluctantly scooted him off and rose to my feet. Picking up the rag, I continued to dust.

I paused when I reached Mr. Thornberry's portrait. His painting was special. If you pushed the two indentations embedded in the top of the frame, a secret door would open in the bookshelf. That door led to a hidden garden.

The indentations were not such a secret anymore. Now that Miss Janice had learned about the garden I saw smudge marks marring the indents on the silky wood. With a bit more lemon oil, I proceeded to polish them off.

Janet ran in, all excited. "I knew I'd find you here," she said. Everyone knew this was my favorite room.

"So what did you find out?" I asked.

"Remember Mr. Dee's stolen car? My cousin got back to me. The story is crazy," she giggle-talked.

"Well, hurry and tell me!"

"They did recover the car. And you're not going to believe the story."

"They found the Lincoln? Where?"

"They found it out by an old hotel. When they pulled up they saw somebody run from the car. They chased after the guy and found him hiding in some bushes."

"Oh, wow. That's amazing!" I exclaimed. "So is the guy under arrest?"

"Nope, he's not."

My mouth must've dropped because Janet looked at me and laughed.

"I know I was shocked, too," she said.

"Tell me how an expensive car like that can be stolen, the person caught, and no arrest was made."

"Because the person was Mr. Dee's son, Mikey."

I actually gasped, which made her giggle even harder. She continued, spinning one thin braid. "And when the police told Mr. Dee that it was Mikey, Mr. Dee said that he would not press charges."

"I see." I didn't see. That was a lie.

"And Mikey had a very interesting story about the situation as well. He said that Mr. Dee told him to go pick up a package."

"A likely story," I scoffed.

Janet shrugged. "Not so unlikely. Mikey had a package addressed to his dad in the front seat."

"So, Mr. Dee forgot about it? He just called to say his car was stolen?"

"That's what Mikey said happened. He said that on the way out or later that day he got into a fight with his father, and his dad called it in."

I raised an eyebrow. "I wonder if that was the reason for the estrangement."

"I can totally see why that would cause bad blood between them."

"I wonder if we can find somebody who works there that might be able to tell us a little bit about their relationship."

"I think that everybody has already found a new job by now since Mr. Dee is gone. They sure wouldn't hang around for Mikey, who has no money. You know, they let go of the chauffeur. I'm not sure if there is any help left. The gardeners have been gone for a while. Have you seen how their grounds look? Horrible. Like a jungle."

Now Lucy stuck her head in. "What's going, ladies?"

"We were wondering if we could find someone at Mr. Dee's manor who might be willing to talk with us."

Lucy's brow furrowed while Janet shrugged. "They probably had to sign confidentiality contracts. They might not be able to say anything out of fear of getting sued. And I'm sure they think that Mikey would be all over that since he needs money."

I ruffled the fur around Hank's ears. "There has to be somebody who will talk. People like having the *in* with nasty gossip."

Lucy started back out of the room. "Let me work on that. I'll see what I can do and get back to you later."

CHAPTER TEN

I headed down the hallway to drop my caddy in the cleaning closet when I heard lovely musical notes fill the air. I washed my hands and listened. The sounds still continued after I finished. Curious, I tracked them down and found myself standing outside of the music room.

Miss Janice sat at the piano. She still hadn't yet dressed and her gossamer dressing coat hung over the back of the bench. Her jutting shoulders showed weight loss and made her appear especially frail. Yet her slender fingers moved across the keys in almost a magical way.

I turned to respect her private moment and managed to run straight into one of the doors.

She stopped with a jarring note and stared over her shoulder, her eyes wide with fear. The expression faded when she saw it was me.

"Come in," she said and beckoned to me.

"I'm so sorry. I'm just on my way to prepare for lunch service."

Almost absentmindedly, she allowed her fingers to pick out more notes on the keys. The result sounded reminiscent of the light burbles of a creek.

"That's beautiful," I said.

She smiled and glanced down. "Music soothes the soul, does it not? I've sat here many times. It started during the first years of my marriage when I realized the child I so desperately wanted was not to be. And I sat here after Henry's funeral. I think music heals. It's kind of like a voiceless prayer. Don't you think?"

I nodded, a lump in my throat, as a desperate urge grew to help this strong woman who had seen so much pain. I had to find who put that terrible ad in the newspaper.

"Tell Cook I'd like chicken salad, if it's not too late," she said and went back to her music score.

"I will," I said and quickly left.

Cook was rolling dough out at the counter when I entered. She smiled in response to my hello.

"Is chicken salad possible for lunch? Miss Janice just asked me to check."

"Of course. I keep some shredded chicken in the fridge for just this request."

The door banged open and Janet came in with a big grin on her face. After our last conversation, I was eager to hear what she'd found.

"Well, now, missy. You look like the basset hound who's gotten into the butter. What's up with you?" Cook pressed a doughnut cutter down on the dough's surface.

"Guess what I have." She wiggled her phone, dancing me to Cook.

Cook patted her round creation and set it on a plate. "It better be a winning lottery ticket with all this hoopla. I swear you act like a girl going to the very first dance."

Janet made a face. "That's not very nice. I found a giant clue to help solve Mr. Dee's murder. Now do you guys wanna know what it is, or what?"

I walked over, holding Miss Janice's lunch tray. "Yes! Who sent it to you?"

Janet showed the screen. On it was a picture of a man behind the wheel of a car, someone I'd never seen before. He did look quite aristocratic though.

What struck me was that both Mr. Dee and this man had their hair parted on the same side and in the same style.

"Who is that?" I asked.

"Remember how Mr. Dee's car was stolen? This was a picture taken earlier that day by a traffic camera."

"Well, give me a gander, then." Cook bustled over. She plucked the phone from my hand like it was a ripe berry from a bush, simultaneously grabbing a pair of glasses that hung on a chain from inside her shirt. "Don't understand how you girls can see things this tiny." She pushed the readers on her nose and her mouth moved like she had a wad of gum.

After a moment she handed it back to Janet, decidedly unimpressed. "That's nobody," she proclaimed and waddled back to the counter.

"What do you mean, nobody?" Janet and I said in unison.

"That's just Christopher. Mr. Dee's nephew."

"Why is he driving the car, then?" Janet asked, staring down at the picture.

"He lives at the manor. He was a lifesaver to Mr. Dee a few years back," Cook said. She carried the plate of doughnuts over to the stove where oil was already bubbling in a cast iron pan. Gently she placed them in.

"A lifesaver huh? So do he and Mikey get along?" I asked.

She blew a stray hair out of her face and nudged her doughnuts apart. "Christopher gets along with everyone. He's a giving guy. He once flew in an emergency donation for a hospital by helicopter. That's what I mean—a lifesaver."

"All right. Quit holding out on us. What happened?" Janet asked.

"He assisted Mr. Dee when he had his last stroke. He has his nursing license and was able to help him recover."

"And that didn't cause complications between him and Mikey?"

"No. Christopher and Mikey have been close ever since childhood. Those two are practically like brothers."

"So, how did Christopher take to Mikey getting into trouble with the check fraud?"

"Christopher has tried to help Mikey at times. But mostly he just accepted him for the way he was. Sometimes you can't change the leopard spots, and you're a better person to know that."

Cook flipped over the donuts, now with golden yellow bellies. After a moment she extracted them, using a wire basket spoon, and let them rest on paper towels while she went back to cutting her dough. As soon as the next batch was frying she dusted the first batch with powdered sugar.

"I'm not sure about those." I stared at the donuts.

Cook's lip worked at the corner. "You trying to tell me there's something wrong with them?"

"Yeah, they don't seem quite the same as you usually make them."

"So, I'm supposing you want to check." Cook put her hands on her hips.

"Well, if you insist." I grinned and reached over to grab one. I glanced at her to be sure it was okay.

Cook laughed and waved her towel. "You're just as bad as a teenager, I swear."

I broke it in half, giving part to Janet, and then popped mine in my mouth. The warm pastry practically melted on my tongue. If there was something wrong with these, the next batch must be made in heaven.

Cook snuck a bite herself.

"So, new question. How can we find out who posted a personal ad?" I asked. Reaching for my phone, I started the search for the newspaper and clicked on the link to submit a classified.

Marguerite came in then. The lines by her lips drew her mouth down, and her entire demeanor felt heavy.

Cook took one glance at her and clucked her tongue. "Good heavens, you look like something the cat dragged in. What's the matter now?"

"Miss Janice. It's just not right, I'm telling you."

Cook nodded her head in my direction while her hands remained busy with cutting dough. "She's trying to find out who did it, you know."

"Good luck, dear one. No one deserves sniper fire from the newspaper like that." Then Marguerite turned to Cook. "I need your help."

"What? Can't you see I'm busy?"

"Busy eating doughnuts! Yes, I saw that. Now come on."

Cook grumbled but wiped her hands. "Watch my oil," she demanded Janet.

Quickly I texted the newspaper. Since I couldn't find a direct match to my question, I ended up sending an email to ask if it were possible to track down the person who placed the ad about Miss Janice. Sometimes it was best to be direct and to the point.

I heard snickering and glanced up to see Janet holding open the door. She had a look of both disbelief and glee, so I had to hop out of the chair to see.

Marguerite and Cook were halfway up the stairs, trying to move the floor buffer. Both of the women's faces were red with effort. Cook's pink headband had slipped down and covered one eye.

I choked back a giggle. I didn't want to be the one caught laughing at them.

"Don't knick the floor, Cook," Marguerite grunted. "Pick your end up higher."

"Are you kidding me? What about my ankles? You nearly clipped them with that crab move you call a walk," Cook shot back.

They made it to the landing by the time I ran forward.

"Can I help?" I asked.

"Oh, don't worry. You're going to be helping plenty," Marguerite said.

Cook cackled as my stomach sank. I disappeared back into the kitchen. With that threat hanging over my head I figured I deserved another doughnut.

CHAPTER ELEVEN

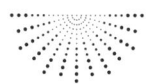

Marguerite wasn't lying. After lunch she sent us girls into the great ballroom to polish the entire, hulking floor.

Initially, it didn't sound that impossible until we were told we had to clean every mark first. That required meticulous attention to detail in order to remove the scuffs on the travertine stone floor.

An hour later and we'd barely covered a quarter of the cold hard area.

"You're going so slow I need a sundial to time you," Jessie said to me in a huff.

I grunted in response. Honestly, the truth hurt. So did my back. And my knees.

Jessie threw her rag to the floor. "Sorry about that. My body feels like a house of cards about to topple over."

"Me too."

"Any more word about who sent the threat into the newspaper?"

"I think it was Mikey." Maybe it wasn't, but after seeing that weird smile he gave me when we drove by I wouldn't put it past him.

She nodded. "Sure. Put the blame on Miss Janice and inherit the estate scot-free. Makes sense to me."

"Why are we assuming that Mikey stands to inherit Mr. Dee's estate?" Mary asked.

"Why wouldn't he?" I asked.

"I mean, he stole Mr. Dee's car. I've heard of people changing their will for a lot less than that." She grunted as she stood up, her face wincing while she stretched her back.

"Real lady-like." Jessie laughed.

"Please. I'm about as ladylike as a giraffe." She waggled her arms and a leg to demonstrate, making me giggle.

"I want to run the buffer," Jessie exclaimed.

"It's all yours, baby." Mary said.

I picked at a particularly stubborn spot. "Considering their falling out, wouldn't that make Mikey the prime suspect?"

"I would think so." Mary wiped her forehead with her arm. She pulled out her phone and started to type.

"Don't let Marguerite catch you doing that," Jessie warned.

Mary shrugged. "Marguerite is nothing like Patty."

A shiver ran through me at the mention of the temporary housekeeper's name.

"Besides I'm looking into the investigation." She read silently for a moment and then said, "See here. There was a press update just last night."

"Isn't a press update kind of dramatic? Aren't people murdered all the time?" Jessie leaned back on her heels.

"Sure, but when your family is a town founder I guess you get special attention." She read, "The police are investigating several leads. Mikey Dee was taken in for an interview to see how he could help this afternoon. We are confident that we are narrowing our leads down, and our evidence points to a certain someone that will make everything clear. We will let you know more in the future, as this case is still sensitive."

"Well, now it does look like they are looking into Mikey as a suspect. It makes sense to me. I wonder where Mikey is today."

Mary's fingers flew over the keyboard, and soon she was smiling. "I don't know about today. But last night he tagged himself at the Purple Pig."

"Purple Pig?" I said.

"Yeah, that's the bar in town."

"I wonder if that's the bar where Lucy's boyfriend works," I asked.

Jessie rose to her feet. "I think we should find out. Where is Lucy today?"

"Marguerite has her in laundry," Mary offered.

"I'll go look for the polish. Maybe it's upstairs," she said with a wink as she headed out.

"Why would it be upstairs?" I asked, scraping at the gummy stain.

"She's kidding," Mary said. She shoved her hair back from her face. "This humidity has my hair going crazy today. And Dylan was going to meet me today."

"Wait a minute. Dylan? Wasn't he the guy you asked about at the dry cleaners?" I asked.

Mary nodded. "He's the one who helped me when I dropped off Miss Janice's pantsuit. The one that huge guy said wasn't there anymore."

"Don't you think you should have told us this a while back?"

"There was nothing to tell," Mary defended hotly. "He only just called me today."

"How did he get your phone number?" I asked.

"I left my number with the contact information."

"Don't you think that's odd he would keep it?"

"I knew you would think it was weird. That's another reason why I didn't want to tell you guys. It's no big deal. He just called to ask me for a coffee. Not everything is suspicious, you know."

"Maybe so, but this whole thing started at the dry cleaners," I said.

She scrubbed the floor furiously. I could tell I'd made her mad. She'd never been mad at me before. I decided to back off and focused on my corner of the floor. We worked in silence for about ten minutes, with me hoping Jessie would come back soon.

Luckily, hard work can sometimes diffuse strong emotions. After another minute, Mary said, "I don't have to see him if you think it's weird."

"I'm not sure what I think. Just be careful, will you?"

"I'm always careful." she grinned. "Remember my spider monkey skills."

Jessie came galloping back down the stairs and skidded on her socks across the floor. "Guess what? Lucy's boyfriend does work there."

Mary stood up and stretched her back. "Well, don't leave us in suspense. What did she say?"

"She texted him, and that's what took us so long. He said that Mikey came in, all blustering. Everyone wanted to buy him a drink. After a few he started talking about how the police had built a case and were very close to getting the suspect."

I frowned. "Suspect? He was happy about it?"

"Very. He said justice was about to be carried out."

Marguerite came bustling around the corner. "What's all that noise?" she demanded.

Mary filled her in.

Marguerite's forehead wrinkles smoothed out. "Well, that's some good news, I suppose. I'd like to put this all to bed so we can move on. Can't be having Miss Janice getting nasty threats in the newspaper forever now can we? It's not good for my soul. It isn't."

I went back to scraping the floor. Marguerite said it was good news. But something in my gut told me we weren't going to be happy about the outcome.

CHAPTER TWELVE

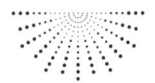

I talked Mary into letting me tag along with her on her coffee date. Something about this guy rubbed me the wrong way. Not only did he work at the dry cleaners but he'd also been in charge of the pantsuit that ended up with the offending receipt.

The place where the date was supposed to take place was on remote side. On one side of the building was a consignment store. I parked my butt in the car with a good Kindle book while she went inside the coffee shop.

She texted me at once to let me know Dylan hadn't yet arrived. I cozied down into my seat in a contented way. I'd get a chance to vet him before he even went in the shop. First impressions and all that, I was happy he was a little late.

Half into my book, I watched out the window for my prey to arrive when I saw the consignment store door open. Out stepped Mikey. My blood went to ice, and I ducked down. Would he remember me or the car?

After a few seconds I peeked out again. He jostled his keys in his hand and was looking at his phone. It was then I noticed his left eye was nearly swollen shut. Black pillowed underneath in an ugly way. As he walked by, I turned my head away.

"Hey!" he called.

I nearly fainted. He did recognize me, after all. My muscles refused to work, and I couldn't look him. I saw his reflection in the coffee shop front window.

He wasn't facing me. "Hey!" he yelled again.

"What's up?" called some man in front of me.

Mikey sauntered forward a few steps. "You have a client who can buy my dad's Lincoln?"

"At Dwayne's Dealership? Is it even yours?"

"Sure. It will be once the will is finalized."

"So wait until then."

"I can't. The thing is, I need the money. Come on, for old times. I worked there for ten years. That has to be worth something."

"What do you need money for?" The other's man's voice was laced with skepticism.

"I need it, that's all."

"Oh! You owe someone, huh?" The tone took a knowing turn. "They did that to you?"

"Don't worry about it." Mikey strode forward.

"Listen, I'll ask the boss and we'll see. You okay, buddy? You don't look so good."

They both turned and walked away together.

I wasn't sure if he would return, so I stayed scrunched in my reclined seat. I'm sure I looked like a sight. I didn't see if Dylan showed up, and I felt too nervous even to read. My neck had a crick in it and my back started to ache. I wasn't built to be a spy, apparently.

As I laid there, I replayed the memory of Mikey exiting the clothing store. Something jumped out to me. The big bag hanging off his arm had been stuffed full of what looked like pink baby items, and there'd been a purple teddy bear tucked under his arm. My mind went immediately to the pregnant woman.

I don't know how long I waited there, tucked down and sweaty. But eventually the door opened and Mary returned.

She didn't look happy.

"How did it go?" I asked, scooting up.

She didn't even ask about my weird position. Instead, she said sadly, "He didn't show up."

I couldn't wait to tell her what I'd seen, but she was too depressed. "I'm sorry. What a jerk."

She started the car and shifted into drive. "This is one of the first times I've struck out. I promise you that. I've only had it happen once, in high school."

I readied myself for a story.

"He was two years older than me, a senior. Everyone wanted him. Everyone wanted to be me."

"And?"

"It was magical. He was so handsome, so attentive. I was so flattered."

I had a bad feeling. I couldn't even make myself prompt her.

"One night he took me on a date out on the river. He was one of those notches in the belt, and I wasn't ready to be a notch. It didn't go well, and I ended up walking home."

"Were you okay?"

Mary's expression gripped my soul. This was a girl who was confident. Funny. A quick thinker. And I was caught off guard by this moment of vulnerability.

"You know, I have a lot of brothers?"

I nodded.

"Problem solved." She said it through a stiff smile. But her misty eyes betrayed her. I leaned over and gave her a half hug, and she allowed it for a second. Then she said. "In other news, are we going to find the guy who dared murder our neighbor or not?"

"Turns out I'm not such a bad spy after all." I grinned, and then shared everything about Mikey.

* * *

Later that night, both Lucy and Mary came up to my room.

"What a day, right?" I asked.

"Poor Miss Janice." Mary had a plate of doughnuts.

"It's scary how he keeps stalking her. And even scarier you saw Mikey today. Do you think we could be in danger?" Lucy asked.

We climbed on my bed where Hank lifted his head, his face fur all rumpled, with disgusted eyes at having his sleep disturbed. Even more upsetting to him, Mary scooted him out of his warm spot to make room for herself. He stared her down the way a lion would a little rabbit, and I realized Mary should be thankful that Hank was the size that he was.

I leaned over and smoothed his fur back and scooted him by my pillow. You would think that being on the cushion would've made him happy. Instead, he jumped off the bed, making it vibrate, and marched hard to the cupboard door where he haughtily disappeared inside.

"Did you learn any more about the bloody handkerchief?" I asked.

"I mean, you don't think Miss Janice would have... really?" Lucy stammered.

I shook my head while Mary adamantly said, "No way."

"Remember our conversation earlier?" Lucy slid off her shoes and curled up even more.

"Which one?"

"The one about finding someone at Mr. D's estate to talk with. I told Mary I think I have someone. Are you ready?" Lucy whispered, pulling out her phone.

I grabbed a doughnut. Mary nodded to answer Lucy. Lucy dialed the number.

"Who is this again?" I whispered.

"It's her friend Jasmine," Mary answered, mumbling around a mouthful of doughnut.

The phone answered, and Lucy waved at us to be quiet. "Hello, Jasmine?"

"Yes?"

"Hi, this is Lucy Terrance." There was no answering reply—instead silence. Lucy continued with only the tiniest bit of a lisp showing her nerves. "We met at Derby Days last summer. My boyfriend and your boyfriend are old friends." She pushed the speaker.

"Max. I dumped him two months ago. That jerk had another girlfriend he didn't think I knew about."

"Oh." Lucy's voice drained as she realized the demise of the companionship bond she thought she shared with Jasmine. Then she perked up. "Well, Larry and I aren't on the greatest terms either."

"Ha." Jasmine did not sound impressed.

"Anyway we've had a little bit of drama in our town. I remembered that you used to work at Mr. Dee's place." Lucy continued as Mary waved her hands to encourage her and gave her a thumbs up.

"So?" Jasmine responded.

This was not going well. I could see Lucy getting flustered. I grabbed a piece of paper and scribbled and then passed it over to her. Lucy glanced at the paper and then said, "I was thinking about working for Mr. Dee. I need a job. I feel like I remember that you used to work there. Is he a good boss?"

Jasmine snorted. "Sure, work there if you want. If you like working for free."

"Free?" Lucy said.

"Yeah, free. Those men are so cheap they probably check under the bed to see if they lost any sleep. I still haven't been paid for my last three months there."

"Oh geez, I didn't know."

"Yeah, it's no surprise Mr. Dee was murdered. But don't tell anybody I said that."

I made a face. That was harsh.

"I wondered if it would be safe to work there. Do you have any idea who might have done it? I heard it was Mrs. Thornberry."

Jasmine breathed heavily. "There's no way Mrs. Thornberry did it. Have you seen the size of her? She is about as big as a stick broom. No, I think we all know who did it."

"Okay? Who is that?"

"Well, Mr. Dee might've been a skinflint, but that's because his son spent all the money. And guess who has some people looking for him now?" Jasmine said.

"What do you mean, people?" Lucy stammered slightly.

"Rumor has it things went south for him at a poker game downtown a while ago. Somebody called in their dues. Trust me, they'll get Mikey to pay. I think they got to Mr. Dee as a warning."

"That's dreadful!"

"Mikey is going to inherit everything. And just in the nick of time too." Jasmine said firmly.

"What do you mean?" Lucy asked.

I reached for another bite of the doughnut, only to discover I'd finished it. This was like a real life soap opera.

"It wasn't that long ago that Mikey nicked Mr. Dee's car. Oh, man, you should've heard the fight when the car was found."

"Wasn't it that Mr. Dee wanted Mikey to pick up a package for him?"

Lucy was doing so well. I was really proud of her.

Jasmine snorted. "That's the rumor they spun. In reality Mikey stole that car. He was going to fence it to pay off his bill. That didn't go over too well with Mr. Dee. When Mikey returned home and the police finally left, they got into a screaming match in the library. We were all listening."

"You could hear him?"

"Hear him! I'm surprised you couldn't hear them down there. Things were broken too. I'm telling you it was a knockout drag-out fight. Mr. Dee told him that he was out of the will. Mr. Dee said he would be in contact with his lawyer in the morning. That's when we heard it get physical."

"Then what did you do?" Lucy gasped.

"Tommy the foreman jumped into the mix. He might have even hit Mr. Dee."

"No!" Lucy gasped.

"Yeah. That's why he got fired. Mr. Dee ended up getting hold of Christopher, asking for help."

"Did Christopher live there?"

"Yeah. He lives down at the pool house. That was another problem because Mr. Dee wanted him to live in the main house, but Mikey wouldn't let him. Mr. Dee always threatened to make Christopher his heir instead of Mikey. You can imagine how well that went over."

"So Mikey and Christopher didn't get along?"

"Not at all. Mikey despises Christopher. And so did Tommy the foreman."

"So, Mr. Dee called Christopher and then what happened?"

"Christopher showed up with his muscles all bulging and stormed into the library. Tommy ran out like a coward. The next thing we knew Christopher was wrestling Mikey by holding his arm behind his back and frog-marched him out of the house."

"Then what?"

"Then cooler heads prevailed and things went back to normal."

"So did Mr. Dee ever contact his lawyer?"

"The next day Mikey came back all contrite and promised he would quit gambling and straighten up. He asked for one more chance. Mr. Dee said he was sick and tired of giving him chances. Mikey begged and said if he screwed up again he wouldn't contest the will. Mr. Dee agreed to that. Mikey signed a paper saying he would not contest the will. It wasn't too long after that I quit. They couldn't pay me enough to stay in that crazy house."

"Thank you, Jasmine, for talking to me. I guess I won't be working there after all." Lucy said.

"That place is a house for yo-yos. Plus the guy always tried to date us girls. I'd get a job at a fast-food restaurant before I ever worked there again." Jasmine said and hung up.

"What do you think about that?"

Mary covered her face. "I think we need to look into Tommy. He didn't like Christopher, hit Mr. Dee, and he was fired. That sounds like a motive to me."

I wrinkled my nose. The last thing we needed was another suspect.

CHAPTER THIRTEEN

As they say, another day, another dollar. This morning found me stinking like a pickle as I stood in front of a streaked parlor window. Marguerite preferred vinegar along with crumpled newspapers to clean the glass, and it was a smelly job. I'd never used vinegar before, and thought she was bananas when she told me. So I was surprised with how it worked. Still, windows were my least favorite chore. Right after toilets. Right after polishing travertine floors.

A screeching metallic noise from outside ripped through the air. I held my breath to listen. Another horrible crash vibrated the floor.

Someone ran past the door with fast, frantic steps. A second set of feet chased after the first. I dropped the paper and spray bottle and ran for the hall myself.

The sounds of more pounding feet came from a different direction. I panicked, wondering what was going on. Then I heard Butler yell, "Go home!"

His words sent shocks down my spine. I peered down the hallway. I didn't see anyone, so I ran for the foyer.

The chandelier splashed little rainbow bits against the walls and floor. I couldn't see the front door where the action was happening. A giant vase of flowers hid the view. I could, however, see a bright square on the marble floor that told me that the front door was wide open. I heard more steps and Marguerite walked briskly from the kitchen to join Butler at the front door.

"Go home, I said!" Butler demanded, his voice growly.

Some man yelled back. "I'm sick of you Thornberrys! Why are you snooping in my life? Do you think you can get away with that?" His angry voice lowered in a threatening way.

"Mikey, you're drunk." Marguerite leaned back on her heels and stood with her arms crossed over her ample chest.

"I'm drunk? I'm not drunk. You're all drunk on the power of trying to ruin a man's life. Wasn't it enough to kill my dad? Now you're trying to take me down, too. Maybe pin the murder on me?"

"We have no idea what you're talking about," Butler said.

"You don't, huh? I think you know exactly what I'm talking about."

Mary skated around the corner of the foyer and stopped next to me. She gripped my arm when she heard Mikey say that.

We knew what he meant. It had to be the conversation that Lucy had with Jasmine. Somehow it had gotten back to Mikey.

That shouldn't have surprised me. We all gossiped like it was going out of style.

A crash came out on the front porch. I closed my eyes and hoped it wasn't the lion statue that stood like a sentinel on the stoop.

"Don't do that, son. I'll have to call the police!" Butler warned. There was another crash of something smashing.

I texted Steve. He needed to come fast to help Butler.

"Go on home, Mikey," Marguerite said sternly. "Don't do anything else you might regret."

Cook scuttled around the corner then. She had the home phone clutched in her hand and was talking vigorously. I figured she must be talking to the police. Desperate times called for desperate actions.

Butler walked out onto the porch now, and his thin, tall body was highlighted for a moment by the bright sky like a skinny scarecrow. He appeared much older as he faced the inebriated man, and I worried. But his spine straightened to show he was not in the least intimidated. I was impressed.

I couldn't hear what Butler said, except it elicited more yelling as a response. Marguerite now joined Butler on the porch and threw her voice into the match.

Mary and I stared at each other. I wondered if we should intervene.

Out of the blue, I heard a fourth voice, a male, and I thought Steve had finally arrived.

It proved to be completely inaccurate as Mikey yelled out, "Christopher! Let me go!"

"Come on, buddy. Let's go home," said the man I now figured was Christopher. He added, "I'm sorry about the trouble, Marguerite and Butler. Let me know what the statue costs. Of course, I'll pay for it. I'll send over Jackson to check out the gate."

Mikey screamed more intensely, but his voice faded in the distance. Then I heard a car door slam and a vehicle drove off.

Marguerite and Butler walked through the door like two soldiers returning from battle. They both eyed each other wearily, and Butler latched the door tightly behind them. His hand dropped to his side.

Butler caught my eye. "Mikey rammed our gate and smashed it open. His jeep is still out there, mangled, I guess. I need to call for a tow."

"You let Christopher handle that," Marguerite snapped. "This isn't our job to fix. We have our own hands full with what the Missus will say when she hears about this. In fact, I better go prepare that headache tonic now."

The back door slammed open and footsteps echoed through the kitchen. Then Stephen popped through the doorway, red-faced and out of breath. His muscles bulged under his shirt and his hands formed into fists. I was impressed that, despite how worked up he was, his eyes were clear and not wild-eyed.

"Where is he?" he asked, his calm voice for some reason even scarier than anger.

"Christopher came by and collected him," Marguerite said, as if Mikey were garbage. "Truth be told, I was surprised to see him here."

Cook readjusted her headband. "I called him."

"That was smart," Butler said. "That could have gone very badly."

"And we certainly couldn't have the police here again, not with what they asked Miss Janice last time. Besides, I knew he'd know what to do," Cook explained.

"What happened?" Stephen asked.

"Mikey came here quite upset because he received word that we were snooping into his business," Butler said.

"And we would never do that. Would we, girls?" Marguerite turned and looked straight at us. Mary grinned weakly while I felt the blood drain from my face. We couldn't get in trouble for asking a few questions, could we?

"Actually, we did run into somebody who used to work there," Mary explained. I loved how she always was the one to jump on the grenade for us. "She simply confirmed what we already knew about Mikey, except to add that he almost got written out of the will over the last mishap he caused. And since then, he supposedly has been walking on the straight and narrow."

"Oh, my goodness, ladies. You sure stirred up a hornet's nest, that's what. You two could get in trouble in a church," Marguerite said, exasperated. Although her facial coloring was returning to normal, two red spots remained on her cheeks.

"Marguerite!" Mrs. Janice's frail voice warbled from upstairs. We all glanced up. She leaned over the top railing. "What was that all about?"

"That was a visit from the neighbor," Butler explained.

"I've got your headache tonic coming right up, Miss Janice," Marguerite said. "I'll explain everything once I'm there."

"Oh, dear," Miss Janice replied. She blinked hard, as if trying to wake up from a bad dream, before turning back to her room. I honestly felt shocked to see the changes in her physical appearance. The stress of the last few days surrounding Mr. Dee's murder weighed on her like a death shawl.

Marguerite thumped up the stairs as Stephen walked over to me. "You okay?"

"I am. Thank you for coming so fast."

"Of course." He studied me, his eyes warm with concern. "You sure you're fine?"

I nodded.

Cook hollered then, "Aren't you out helping the new worker?"

Stephen's chin jerked and then he nodded. He rubbed the back stubble of his neck, waved at me, and left by the front door.

"New worker?" Mary asked, holding an extra nonchalant tone.

Cook narrowed her eyes. "The kid's name is Thomas. I think you'll meet him at lunch. Try not to climb all over him."

Mary put her hands on her hips. "Cook! What makes you think I'd climb all over someone? I have standards, you know."

Cook harrumphed. "Don't be giving me that, missy. As long as the man has a heartbeat, a nice smile, and one of those senses of humor, you're on him like bees on honey."

"Please!" Mary stamped her foot. "I don't go after everyone."

"She's never gone after Butler," Lucy offered helpfully.

We all laughed with the exception of Mary. Butler peered from the back room, his dour-faced pulled into a decided frown.

"Get on with you ladies. I'm sure you have chores." Cook waved her towel. I reluctantly returned back to the parlor to finish the windows. Vinegar, here I come.

CHAPTER FOURTEEN

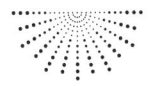

I knew how fast gossip flew around in this manor, but I was surprised to discover it moved just as fast in a small town. The afternoon sun hadn't yet stretched the trees' shadows over the front lawn before Jessie popped into the morning room where we were cleaning windows.

"Did you hear what they're saying?" Jessie asked.

"Who?" asked Mary.

"There's talk over at the store about Mikey coming here and breaking in the gate. And everyone said that Miss Janice deserves it!" Jessie's indignant eyes reminded me of a cat's.

"You're kidding me? Why? They think she's responsible for Mr. Dee's death?"

Jessie nodded. "Yep. They say poison is a woman's method of murder and those two have had that property line squabble for years now."

"That stupid property line." I arched an eyebrow at Mary. "You do know what we have to do, don't you?"

"Let me guess. You're dragging me back to that old church aren't you?"

"I think that's where it all ends, Mary."

"If..." She held up a finger. "...and I mean a very vague *if* we were to find some kind of treasure, how would that let Miss Janice off the hook? It seems it makes her motive even stronger."

"I understand, but that's where it all began," I said.

"Wait!" Mary raised another finger for her new point. "Tell me how this strengthens the motive for Mikey?

"I don't know," I said, rubbing my neck. She had a point. "But—"

"Wait! I'm not done yet. That still doesn't answer our biggest question."

"And what's that?"

"The gas station receipt that we found in Miss Janice's pocket. How did that get there?"

Jessie laughed. "It's not because she followed him there and murdered him. She's grumpy sometimes when she doesn't get her headache tonic, but there's no way she'd ever stoop so low as to do this. Besides, why would she get her hands dirty when she could just hire somebody?"

Mary snorted. "That's true. Rich people like to hire people."

"Obviously someone wanted to pin the murder on Miss Janice," I said.

"The dry cleaner did go to the police," Mary said thoughtfully.

I nodded. "Exactly. And why didn't they call the police sooner? Maybe because they thought we wouldn't discover it and it would still be there for the police to find."

Mary finished wiping her window. "Here's another theory. She was wearing that jacket at the gala. Do you think somebody could've just stuck it in her pocket?"

"Maybe. But someone like who?" Jessie sat back on her heels. Hank had popped out of somewhere and was heading straight for her.

"We need a confession," I told Mary.

"Don't we all," she sighed.

"I'm serious. Wouldn't it be great?"

"Tell me who to ask."

"Who else has a motive?" Jessie patted Hank's head, who gave her an appreciative cheek rub.

"I'm not sure? And they said he drank it, which is very unfortunate since they had that drink in her town car." Mary sighed.

Marguerite peeked in. "Ladies, as if my day isn't a mess enough, I don't have any time for you to be lollygagging. Come on down now and start making sandwiches."

"What's the matter?" I asked.

"Miss Janice has had another bloody nose. I guess that's what happened the night of the gala, when Janet found her handkerchief. At any rate, it's everywhere. Now, hurry up. I think the outside crew will be in here soon."

"Is the new guy nice?" Mary asked hopefully.

"I guess you'll have to wait and see," Marguerite answered smartly and strode away, her heels clicking against the floor.

We tidied everything up and headed downstairs. Once in the kitchen, I pulled out meat, cheese, pickles, and sandwich condiments while Mary sliced a loaf of bread. We worked like a conveyor belt, with Jessie spreading the mayonnaise, I added the meat and cheese, and Mary topped with pickles and a piece of bread. Lucy came over and cut them and assembled them on a plate.

The back door banged, and Stephen and an attractive, thin young man came stomping through the back door. Stephen must have been working hard because his arms were scratched, and when he took his hat off it revealed a mop of sweaty hair.

"Wash your hands!" Cook screeched.

The two men headed to the butler's pantry and splashing could be heard. Mary gawked with a thoughtful expression. She caught me watching her.

"What?" she asked defensively. And then she grinned. "He's a cutie."

"Mary!" Marguerite warned.

"I'm being good!" Mary lifted her hands. She noticed a spot of mustard on her finger and licked it off before smiling wickedly at me.

At the approaching footsteps, her face fell into an innocent expression again. Stephen opened the cupboard where he retrieved two glasses. Handing one to the young man, he said, "Thomas, this is Cook, Marguerite, and the girls. This is Thomas." He dipped his head toward the newcomer.

We all said hi, but Mary rushed forward with her hand out. "I'm Mary," she simpered.

I nearly laughed. I'd never seen Mary as anything but calm, cool and collected. This was one for the books. I don't think Thomas knew what storm was coming.

CHAPTER FIFTEEN

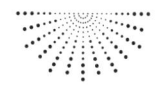

That night at bedtime, Hank climbed on my lap and, in the process, blocked my view of the phone. He sniffed the screen. I swear he wanted to see what was so interesting that stole my time away from him.

Mikey needed money, didn't he? I remembered the desperate expression on his face when he tried to sell the car. And that black eye….I sighed, and Hank licked my finger.

Dwayne's Dealership. Mikey said he had been there for ten years. I decided to reach out to the manager. Maybe I could pretend to be hiring Mikey and was searching for a referral.

I checked the time. Nine o'clock was pretty late, but I figured I could leave a message. I looked up the number for the manager, a guy named Carl, and made the call. As it rang, it occurred to me this guy could be the man Mikey met with earlier. That would be awkward, and I rethought the message wording.

Surprise jolted through me when a man answered the phone. "Carl, here."

"H-hello," I stammered, my little script erasing from my head. "I didn't expect anyone to answer."

"You called me, I answered. We have late hours in the summer."

"Oh, I see." His voice sounded different than Mikey's friend's. It gave me the bolster I needed to bluff like crazy. "Mike Dee left your name as a reference. I wanted to ask you about his character as a work reference."

"Wow. I'm surprised Mikey used me as a referral."

I winced. I should have realized Mikey left the job poorly. There was nothing to do but to forge ahead and keep up the sham. "So it says here that he worked there two years ago?"

"Two years? That's it? I feel like it was much longer than that."

"I see." Strike two. I struggled to come up with the next question. Lucky for me, Carl carried on.

"Good ol, Mikey." He chuckled. I eased out a breath and felt hopeful. "He wasn't all that bad. In fact, in the beginning, his performance was quite impressive. I had every expectation he would move right up in the company."

"Really?"

"Sure, he was always on time, informative, inventive. The guy took care of himself, too, in shape, health-conscious. Used to nag me about my fast food meals."

That had me cringing since it didn't match the man I saw staggering about on the front porch. "Really? Did he drink?" There it was, smooth me giving up more information than a prospective boss ought to know.

Luckily, Carl didn't catch on.

"Yeah, we'd go out for a few after work. All of us guys did. It was a great way to let off some steam after dealing with customers all day. But he never let it get out of hand, other than a few losses at pool."

"So why isn't Mikey there now?"

"Usual story. Personal problems. In the end, his troubles brought him down. They turned out to be more than he could handle."

"I see. His family?"

Now he was catching on. "What's it to you?"

"We have a good counseling program. Maybe it can help."

"Don't think you can help him with his problem unless you can bring his fiancé back."

I straightened up, nudging Hank. He lashed his tail but otherwise didn't move. This was news. "What happened to her?" I covered my eyes, expecting the worst.

"She left him."

I relaxed a bit and reached down to stroke Hank's cheek. Well, that wasn't as bad as I thought. Still, "She left him? Was it the drinking?"

"The drinking came later. Honestly, I was shocked. I thought they got along great, and he seemed like he had it all. She wanted kids. He wanted kids, too. I guess they'd been trying for a while and went in for one of those tests." Here his voice twisted sarcastically to show what he thought about tests. "And it came back that he couldn't. So then she left him. Completely destroyed the guy."

The revelation hit me hard. I suddenly felt terrible for him. The guy wanted a family and found out he couldn't and then had to endure the love of his life abandoning him. I hadn't been prepared to feel sorry for Mikey.

"Yeah," Carl continued. "It wasn't long after that that Mikey hit his first real gambling debt. Since then, it was almost a free-fall. You never know what's truly in a person until they're tested, that's for sure."

I thanked Carl for his time and hung up. Leaning over, I rested my cheek lightly on Hank's side. He sniffed my hair and sneezed.

"So this guy had a bad fall in his life. But was it so far down that he killed his own dad?" I sat up. Hank blinked half-closed eyes at me before yawning, exposing a miniature lion's mouth. I touched his toes, which he immediately pulled back with an affronted expression.

Sighing, I rolled over and turned out the light.

CHAPTER SIXTEEN

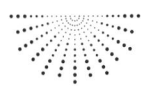

"Well now, isn't this sweet? Restores my faith in humanity," Cook announced at breakfast the next morning. She blew on her cooling tea, pushing swirls of cinnamony-herb scent through the air.

I finished assembling Miss Janice's tray while Cook perused the social section of the morning paper, before I brought that up as well. After the event the other morning, we all kept an eye out for any unpleasant threats in the personal section to spare Miss Janice.

"What's that?" Marguerite asked in between bites of her muesli. Her brow wrinkled as she worked on a particularly crunchy bite.

"One of those pay it forward deals. Some stranger paid for an older couple's meal at Cowboy Vista last Friday." Cook continued to read. "Can you believe this happened on the same night as the gala?" She clicked her tongue. "Just when you're sure the world is lost."

Cook refolded the paper. She heaved herself to her feet with a heavy breath and then walked over to the stove where she started Miss Janice's egg-white omelet.

Mary hurried by with the lemonade pitcher.

"What are you doing?" I asked Mary. I clipped the white rosebud and stuck it in a tiny vase.

"I am bringing two thirsty men something to drink. Because I'm a nice person." She blinked innocently at me.

"Really? What's actually going on?" I asked.

"Jackson came over today to fix the lion statue."

"Jackson as in the Dee's new foreman?"

"Yep. And guess what?"

"What?"

"Christopher came with him." She smiled smugly.

"I see. So you're going to bring them something to drink. So polite. We'll ignore the fact you're about to trick them into giving up some information," I tacked on.

"You know me so well." She checked her hair in the reflection of the sideboard mirror, smoothed back a stray wisp, and then picked up the dewy glasses.

"Hang on a second," I said. I found a plate and covered it with several of Cook's fresh chocolate chip cookies.

Cook snorted when she saw me do it. "Going with a bribe, are you?"

"Didn't you once tell me something about honey draws more bees than flies?"

Cook snorted louder. "You butchered that saying, girlie. You hurry up. These eggs will be done, soon."

I didn't have time to clarify since Mary left me. I hurried after her and caught up just as she stepped out the back door. We walked around the house on the lovely brick walkway that was shaded from the sun by a giant oak tree.

We found the two men out by the front porch.

"Gentlemen!" Mary called cheerfully.

One of the men in gray overalls held the lion's poor broken paw. The other one stood to one side, watching. Of course, I studied Christopher as much as one could politely manage. This was the first time I'd ever seen him in person. I was surprised to see that Christopher wore a dress-down version of a suit, different than the uptight attire I'd expected from the aristocrat. He was incredibly handsome and smiled at us with warm eyes. Hazel, I noticed, and thickly framed with dark eyebrows. Chiseled jaw and perfect teeth.

"Ladies," he said with a nice smile.

The other man worked with a trowel and some type of cement and had already begun repairs on the lion's foot.

"You've got this, Jackson?" Christopher asked.

Jackson grunted that he was doing okay, so Christopher walked towards us.

"We thought you might be thirsty," Mary said and thrust out the tray holding the drinks.

"And needing a snack," I hastily followed with my plate of cookies.

He smiled harder, causing a cute crinkle at the corners of his eyes. He seemed like the type of guy who would work at a mechanic's shop. Someone good-natured, slightly plump but strong and reliable. Someone who was kind to animals.

"Thank you," he said and accepted the glass. He took a long sip, and I watched his Adam's apple bob. "Mmm. That's good." He turned to Jackson. "When you're ready, they have a snack for us."

"I just need to hold this here until the bond sets," Jackson answered. He supported the lion's paw like he was shaking hands with it.

"I am sorry about what my cousin did," Christopher said, dipping his head sadly.

"It was pretty scary," Mary said, managing to look every bit like a damsel in distress. I narrowed my eyes at her suspiciously. That woman could fend off a grizzly bear.

"Yeah, I'm sorry he scared you." Christopher's eyes sparkled with admiration. Now it was my turn to be skeptical. Were they flirting right in front of me?

"You were so brave to get him in the car so fast," Mary simpered.

I had to look up at the trees to choke back a laugh. Mary sure could lay it on thick.

"Yeah. It's too bad he was drinking. Sometimes he gets that way. Tensions are kind of high, after what happened to his dad and all."

"Oh." Mary's eyes rounded like a fawn's. "I'm so sorry. It's me who should be apologizing for your terrible loss."

Christopher kicked at a stub of grass with his sneaker. "It's been a hard adjustment."

"It can't be any easier with Mikey being one of the suspects," Mary said bluntly.

"That would be bad, except it's all cleared up now," Christopher said.

"It is?" I asked, surprised.

Christopher barely glanced at me. I could see that next to Mary's beauty I scarcely caught his attention.

"Yeah," he answered. He casually took a cookie from the plate I held. "When the cops came to interview him, he had an alibi."

"He did?" Mary asked. "I mean, of course he did. I'm not surprised."

"That's so good to know," I said.

"Sure. He was with me that night. We were having dinner."

Mary's forehead wrinkled, but she didn't say anything. So I said it for her. Maybe not the wisest move, but I had to know. "Did you go to the gala?"

Christopher nodded again and shoved a bite of cookie into his mouth. We had to wait until he was finished.

Finally he answered. "Yeah. Afterward, we went to a steakhouse and had a quick dinner. The food at the gala just wasn't enough. All fancy hors d'oeuvres and stuff. Who can get full on a thimbleful of food? Anyway, I showed the police the transaction on my credit card for the meal. Luckily, there was a timestamp. So now they're still looking." At this his cheeks colored. I realized he remembered that one of the suspects was our very own Miss Janice.

"I'm sure the police will figure it out soon," Mary said. I was glad she could talk because my mouth felt like sawdust.

"Oh, they will. I've heard the police are closing in fast."

I didn't know how to handle that kind of information, so I politely smiled and set down the plate on the porch.

"I have to get back," I told Mary. I didn't want to leave her out there alone, but I couldn't handle it anymore.

Mary nodded and placed the other cup next to the plate of cookies. "All right, well, thank you for the repairs."

"Of course. The new gate should be arriving by truck tomorrow. I'll have someone install it, and then we'll be out of your hair. Again, I'm so sorry. I've talked with Mikey, and I promise this will never happen again."

Mary lifted her hand to say goodbye and then we went back around the house.

I felt decidedly less happy now. "Is that the same restaurant Cook was reading about this morning?" I asked. "I wonder if the server remembers those two. Maybe Mikey looked agitated or something."

"Like you think she'll say he looked guilty? You still think he did it, don't you?"

I nodded.

The day continued on, and I was quite curious about all the events of the morning. I couldn't wait until I had a minute to myself to do some investigating.

CHAPTER SEVENTEEN

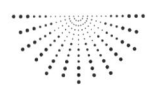

"Ready to scoot?" Mary asked me while pulling on a jacket. The sky was dark and stormy again, and the temperature had dropped.

I checked the time. "You think we can make it to the restaurant and back in an hour?"

"Yeah, but we need to hurry."

Lighting jagged across the sky, followed by thunder that felt like it reached into my chest and squeezed my heart. We ran to the car.

Our plan was to find the waitress who had been working the night of the gala. Maybe, with the right prompting, she'd remember something about Mikey's disposition that night. The news story seemed like the perfect cover.

However, when we arrived, our plan kind of shriveled. We saw someone go inside—Jackson, the Dee's new foreman. He paused as he grabbed the door handle, his shirt tightening over his arm, and searched down the sidewalk. I turned away before we could make eye contact. A second later, he was inside.

Of course, we couldn't very well waltz in there now with our questions, so we stood across the street from the entrance.

"What do we do?"

Mary unpeeled a piece of gum and stuck it in her mouth. "I guess we wait."

A woman approached behind Mary. She had on knee high boots, a cute leather jacket, and long straight, enviably shiny black hair.

"Mary! How are you?" she called.

I sucked in a breath. The absolute one thing you never wanted to hear when trying to remain incognito was another person shouting your name.

Mary blew a small bubble that snapped. "Let me handle this," she whispered. "Hi, Tina! Long time no see. What are you up to?"

"What am I up to? What are you doing, hiding out around here like a stalker?" the brunette teased.

"Looking for a creeper. He might have been following us."

The woman's eyes narrowed, and she stared around. "Where is he?"

"He went into that cell phone store over there." Mary pointed.

We watched for a few minutes until a single man came out. He was on his phone and must have felt our eyes on him. He glanced our way and smiled. Tina glowered back at him. I shrank, feeling awful for the innocent man.

The guy seemed to take it in stride, because he went back to his phone and walked to his car. Moments later, he drove off.

"All clear, then," Mary said. She shot me a guilty grimace.

"Are you sure you're good?" Tina darted a glance around. "I have my jobber."

"Whats a jobber?"

"This." Tina pulled out a key chain on which dangled a bright pink flat object.

"Oh, cute," I said politely.

"It is cute. Especially the sound it makes." With that, she pulled a trigger and the thing snapped.

I jumped back, and she laughed.

Mary glanced at the restaurant before giving Tina a smile. "Well, it was nice running into you. We probably should finish our errands."

Tina waved and continued down the street, shuffling her purse higher on her shoulder.

"Jackson left while we were talking. He had take-out, thank heavens. You ready?" Mary nodded at the restaurant.

"Let's go."

Mary spit her gum back in the wrapper and wadded it up.

We walked into the restaurant and into another world. They weren't joking about the name, Cowboy Vista. Nearly everyone in here wore cowboy hats, including the patrons.

A gal with a red handkerchief around her neck, a checked shirt, and tight denim jeans sauntered up to us. "Howdy, partners," she drawled. "Just two of you for lunch?"

Mary gave an assertive grin. "Hi, there. Actually, I have a quick question for you. I saw a post in the newspaper regarding an event that happened here last week."

"Okay?" The woman raised her eyebrows, clearly not knowing where we were going.

"So the story we heard happened the other night when someone paid for a meal for another couple."

The lady's eyebrows relaxed, and she nodded with a smile "Oh, yes. Wasn't that nice?"

"Were you here that night?" Mary asked.

"No. That was Susanna."

"Oh, that's right," Mary nodded as if she knew that.

"She works every Wednesday and Thursday night. Usually she doesn't work on Fridays but that night we actually traded shifts. My Henry needed to get some medicine. He'd been feeling off for a few days, and I was really worried. But it all ended well."

"Is Henry okay?" I asked.

"Yes, he's fine. It turned out that he had some of the neighbor's barbecue and found some old chicken skin. It did not agree with him."

I listened to this whole conversation with confusion. I still wasn't a hundred percent if Henry was a child, a man, or an animal.

Mary must've felt the same way because she asked, "Who is Henry, again?"

"My great Dane. That daft animal will eat anything, but sometimes it comes back to bite him in the rear like it did last Friday."

"I'm glad he's better. Is Susanna here now?"

"Yes, that's her over there." And the server pointed.

Standing in that direction was a thin girl in her mid-20s. She had on enough makeup to cover a clown quartet, with inch-long fake spider-leg eyelashes and dirty brown slashes of bronzer.

"Do you think we could talk to her?" Mary asked.

"What? Like do an interview with her or something?"

Mary smiled. "Yes. Exactly right. We'd like to interview her."

The waitress's forehead wrinkled with concern. "You want to come back when she's on lunch?"

I hadn't thought of that. Susanna might not be able to talk until her break time. We certainly couldn't be waiting around for that to happen.

"Can you find out when she's free?" I asked.

The waitress nodded. "Let me go check." Her eyes squinted. "You know, she only has that one table over there. I could probably watch it for her while she talks to you for a minute or so, provided nobody new comes in."

"That would be wonderful. Thank you," Mary said.

She walked behind the counter, grabbing a coffee carafe along the way, and spoke with the other waitress. Susanna glanced over at us curiously. The other waitress nudged her in our direction and took over filling a glass with ice. Susanna wiped her hands on a towel and came over toward us.

"Hi, there," she said with a very friendly smile and a tip of her cowboy hat.

"Hi, I'm Mary." Mary held out her hand. Susanna shook her hand and then glanced at me.

"I'm Laura Lee," I introduced myself.

She shook my hand as well and then said, "This is regarding the post I made?"

"Yeah! The one where the people paid for the other couple's dinner."

"I didn't think that would qualify for a second interview," Susanna said. "Who did you say you were with again?"

There was the question I'd been afraid she'd ask. Mary, however, didn't skip a beat. "We are with a library club."

"A library club." She said it like she was tasting a flavored coffee. "That sounds great." Her face relaxed. "So it's just a casual thing, then?"

"Just a little story for a small group. But it's so heartwarming, and with these dark days, we could use all the good news we can get."

"Sure. It's no problem." Susanna then told the same story Cook had read this morning.

I had a few questions ready to fire off about the other people she saw that night when one of her comments stopped me cold.

"Can you repeat the last thing you said?" I asked.

"Sure. The man rushed in and waved me down. He asked to pay for the couple."

I swear my skin shivered. "You mean the guy who paid wasn't here eating all along?"

"Nope. He looked around the restaurant for about ten seconds and then pointed the couple out. He said he'd like to pay for the meal. He was very clear that he wanted a receipt."

"And you have no idea who he was?"

"Nope. But there was one very obvious thing about him. That red plaid jacket of his."

CHAPTER EIGHTEEN

Anger fueled each of my stomping steps as I returned to the car. "I knew it was Mikey!" I couldn't believe I'd felt sorry for him the night before.

Mary slid into the driver's seat. "So he found himself an alibi!"

"What about Christopher? He said he was there too."

"Obviously, his cousin was lying for him. But why?"

"The whole blood is thicker than water thing." I stared out the window, still fuming. "He tricked me."

"Who tricked you?"

"Mikey." I filled her in with the phone call with his old boss the night before, and how I'd learned his life had fallen apart after his fiancé left him.

"Weird," she said. And her brow wrinkled.

"What?"

"Well, wasn't he hanging out with a pregnant lady when we were searching for the library?"

I remembered. "And they seemed awful chummy."

"Very. I thought they were together. You think things," she raised her eyebrows. "Fixed themselves? And he's finally going to be a daddy?"

I shrugged. I had no idea.

She started the car. "I say we take a little trip to the dry cleaners and talk to her."

"Do we have time?"

She glanced at the clock and grimaced. "Barely. Let's go."

"How are we going to find her?" I asked.

"You just leave that to me." Mary shifted her shoulders back, confidently.

We walked into the dry cleaner's, and the big guy who helped us last time came out of the back room. His eyebrows scrunched together and his lips curled in a decidedly angry way as he recognized us. I didn't like how he looked at us.

"You again?" he growled. His biceps flexed like two cantaloupes as he waited for an answer.

Mary came through as smooth as a woman selling Avon. "Why, hello, there! I'm Mary, and my sister runs a baby boutique. She was just saying she had an overrun on some infant clothing and asked if I knew anyone who was pregnant. Of course, I thought of the young girl that works here."

"Lydia? How do you know her?"

Mary continued to schmooze. "Lydia's amazing! She saved a sweater of mine, and she's just so sweet. I'd love to be able to gift the clothes to her. Is she around?"

He lifted his chin and studied us for what felt like an eternity. I swear I started sweating. He nodded. "I'll go get her."

I could have cheered right then. I was so relieved.

He disappeared into the back, and I heard whispering. She was quiet and he was louder. There was no missing the urgency in his tone.

The young woman came out a moment later. Her round face was pinker than the last time I'd seen her. Her eyes caught us and widened. Did she recognize me from when we drove by?

"You wanted to talk with me?"

"Hi, there," Mary greeted with her freckly, disarming smile. "Did he tell you why we were here?"

Lydia's hand went to rest on the top of her stomach as light as a butterfly. "Dario said you had some baby clothes?" Her eyes looked hopeful. I mentally began tallying my extra money to buy her clothes. How much were baby clothes, anyway?

"That's right! Do you know if you're having a boy or a girl?" Mary asked.

"A girl." She smiled.

"Wonderful!" Mary went on with her lie. I saw my budget expanding along with Lydia's smile.

I really wanted to get her alone to ask a few questions without her boss breathing over our shoulders. I decided to pull a Mary and try to get her outside. "Can you come with me for a moment? I left my phone in the car and I'd like to get your number."

She glanced over her shoulder and then nodded. "Sure. Okay."

CHAPTER NINETEEN

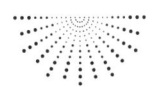

*S*ometimes, when I feel nervous to say something, the words pop out of my mouth in the most awkward way. This was no exception. "Are you dating Mikey?"

She giggled and tossed her ponytail. "Mikey Dee? We really just started hanging out. He's been super nice."

My eyes were drawn to her stomach when she said that. Her belly looked a little bit further along than "just met."

"I see. I thought I saw you with him the other day," I said.

She nodded, her dark eyes wide and sincere. "He's been a good friend. He was returning my jacket from when we saw each other Friday night."

"Wait, you saw him last Friday?" I asked. Will the surprises ever stop?

"Yes. Nearly all evening. I had a couple of appointments and needed a ride. Not only did he take me to each one, but he waited the two hours until it was finished and then brought me back home. He even got me a burger along the way. We didn't get home until late."

"How late is late?"

Lydia stared at the sky like the answer was up there. "Hm, maybe around ten thirty. Like I said, it was a long day, and he's a lifesaver. He even got the baby a teddy bear."

Mary asked for Lydia's number and typed it in. I wanted to ask how he knew she needed a ride, but we were interrupted.

Dario came through the front door. He looked liked a peacock, puffing his chest out. "Lydia! You coming back now?"

She glanced over her shoulder and then at us. With a shy smile, she said, "Okay, you have my information. I look forward to hearing from you."

She darted back inside as fast as a pregnant lady could move.

Mary shook her head. "Nothing's adding up. Do you think she was telling the truth that she and Mikey weren't dating?"

"Maybe she meant they broke up?" I asked. "He was buying baby clothes and that teddy bear. That seems strange for a new friend to do."

Mary shrugged. "She showed zero signs of being angry. I think if I was pregnant by somebody I'd be angry with them and not want to give them an alibi."

"I wish we had a chance to ask her about the receipt in the pocket. That guy has more alibis than anyone I know."

Mary glanced down at her phone. "Starting with the bartender at the gala. Remember, he saw Mr Dee and some guy at the bar?"

"Let's find Lucy and see if she'll ask her boyfriend what time he served Mr. Dee and his friend."

Plan in motion, we raced home.

* * *

I WAITED for the girls to show up later in my room, spending the time on a sketch of Hank. He was the perfect subject. He never moved, not even to twitch a whisker.

A knock came on my door. I hollered, "Come in!"

Lucy led with a plate, which I immediately locked eyes on.

"What's that?" I asked.

"I made my special snickerdoodle cookies," Lucy said.

"You always bring the best treats."

"I'm a treat girl. Every day my mom would set out a snack after school. We didn't have a lot, but I never knew. Sometimes it would be tortillas with cinnamon and sugar. Sometimes it would be buttered saltine crackers."

"Sounds yummy." I said.

"Right?"

Mary turned away. "None for me, thanks. I don't feel that great."

"Aw, I'm sorry. What happened?" I asked.

"I don't know. I thought I made myself car sick. All I can tell you is lunch was better the first time."

I made a face. They approached the bed as if to settle like sparrows landing on a nest. At least Lucy did. Mary tripped on her way and landed on the bed next to Hank like a load of wet towels. At the jolt he lifted his head, his cheek fur all smooshed to one side. His tail lashed angrily as he glared at Mary.

"I didn't do it," she said, holding her hands up. "Have you had a chance to contact your boyfriend? We have more questions for him."

Lucy broke a cookie in half and stuffed a bite in her mouth. She chewed for a few seconds before mumbling around it, "We're taking a break."

"Oh no!" I said.

"What happened?" Mary asked.

"I found out he has more than one girlfriend."

"What a jerk. How do you find that out?"

Lucy picked up her phone and started scrolling. After a second she showed us. Mary grabbed it and began reading it out loud. —**Found your guy with my girlfriend.** And under that was a picture of the couple kissing.

"Oh yuck," Mary said.

"So I can't call him. I swore I'd never talk to Larry again."

Mary closed her eyes. I could tell she was thinking.

"What if one of us calls and pretends we lost a purse at the bar?" I asked.

Mary's eyes popped open. "Laura Lee, you are a genius."

"What was that again?" I asked with a grin.

Mary ignored me and held out her hand. "Give me your phone."

I narrowed my eyes at her.

"What? I can't exactly use Lucy's. He'll know who it is, so give me your phone."

I handed it over and watched her search up the bar's phone number.

"Hello, is Larry there?" Mary asked when the phone finally answered.

"This is him."

"I called the other day, asking about who bartended Friday night." Her lie was as smooth as butter. She continued, "And somebody gave me your name. I left my purse there. Have you seen it?"

We could barely hear him. "Where were you seated?"

"I was close to the front."

"By the guy in the red plaid jacket?"

I almost fell off the bed. I don't know how Mary held it together to calmly answer, "Uh huh. And he was with another man. Remember them?"

There was a pause. "Yes, I do. But I didn't see you there."

"I was kind of in the back."

"With that crowd of women? The Emerald Girls? Okay, yeah. Anyway, sorry, didn't find your purse." He sounded ready to hang up.

"Wait just one sec!" Mary begged. "I have one last question. Could you give me any information about that guy in the jacket?"

"Information?" He sounded wary.

"I feel like he might have picked up my purse."

"I don't think that he would be interested in your bag."

"Call it woman's intuition. I've been getting weird phone calls. I think he has my phone," she said sweetly.

The bartender's voice immediately softened at Mary's honeyed tone. "He seemed pretty focused on the conversation with the other guy. They were arguing about how the young guy got mineral rights for the property. There was other stuff too. All I know is that the guy stormed off, and I can tell you he didn't have a purse. The last I saw, he was leaving in his Jeep."

I nodded. We knew that Mikey had a jeep. It was hauled away from our front gate just this morning.

"What time was that? Are you sure it was him?"

"Probably around nine. I couldn't miss him." Larry laughed. "You should've heard him trying to start his jeep. It took him a while to get out of the parking lot."

"Why?"

"He kept stalling the vehicle. I swear it was must've been the first time he ever drove a clutch before."

"Was it because he was drunk?"

"No," the bartender answered. "Didn't take more than one sip of his beer. And that was after the two guys clinked glasses."

"Clinked glasses?"

"They were celebrating something. That was after the old man came back from the bathroom. A minute later, they were arguing. We all heard it. Even the crowd at the pool table. Then the guy got up and left for his jeep."

"I see," Mary said. "Well, thank you for your help."

"Hey, you sound really cute. Are you single?"

Mary covered her mouth to stifle some judgmental snorts. "I am."

"What's say we get together for a little meet and greet."

She gagged herself with her finger before sweetly speaking into the phone. "Sounds great."

"Tomorrow afternoon at Purple Pig?"

"See you there!"

They hung up.

"Great," I said glumly as she handed back my phone. "Now he's going to call me when no one arrives."

"Well, you'll know what number to block in that case." She laughed.

Lucy rolled her eyes, and pet Hank's back. "What a jerk. He makes me want to hurl."

Mary waved her hand in front of her face. "No talking about hurling, thank you very much."

I leaned back on the bed, trying to pieced together this guy's night. Did he rush there after dropping off Lydia? The time just doesn't match. When did he go to the restaurant? Did he have this drink right before he killed his dad?

CHAPTER TWENTY

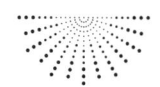

"Why do you think Mr. Dee would meet Mikey at the bar anyway? He threatened him to never drink again," I asked.

"It's very weird. Mike must have doctored the drink when Mr. Dee went to the bathroom. And after that they clinked glasses to celebrate," Lucy said, still petting Hank. His back skin twitched at her touch, like trying to remove a fly.

"Celebrate what? Killing his dad? Evil little twit," Mary mumbled.

"Was it because of the baby? Lydia said he just got back from dropping her off. Maybe he did it for her."

"I want to know what kind of poison works that fast. That's driving me crazy," Lucy said.

I reached for my sketchpad and pencil and started doodling. "What would be the motive for Mikey to frame Miss Janice?"

Mary answered, "That's the million dollar question." I gave her a look. She laughed. "Sorry. They threw the suspicion on her because she seemed to be a likely candidate. Then they'll never get caught."

I stroked Hank with the pencil. "Yes, and Lydia gave him an alibi."

"But why would he need an alibi from Lydia if he already had the fake alibi from Christopher at the restaurant?"

I chewed on the end of the pencil. My picture right now consisted of a lot of mindless doodles and circles, along with my name in cursive letters. Next to it was a sketch of a funny little man. "I think we need to talk to Lydia again."

"Yeah, when Dario's not around. Her boss gives me the creeps. And did you see his eyebrows! Holy cow! A whole herd of crows could nest in them." Mary's own eyebrows raised.

I burst out laughing and shook my head. "I don't think they're called a herd."

"Nope. They're called a murder." Mary fell over on the bed, laughing.

"How long have you been waiting to pull that one out?" I asked.

She laughed. "Come on. It was perfect." She stared at her phone and tapped the screen. "I could call her."

"Well, what do we have to lose?" I shrugged.

"True." She dialed the number.

With each ring, my stomach dropped a little further. I realized Lydia might have given us a fake number.

She hung up. "I guess that's a dead end." She had hardly set the phone down when it rang. It was from that number. Lydia.

Mary snatched it up. "Hello?" she asked breathlessly.

"This is Lydia."

"Hi, Lydia. This is Mary. I'm so glad to hear from you."

"I had to go in the back room to make this phone call. Is it important? Can you make it quick?" It was then I noticed she was whispering.

"I'm sorry I don't wanna get you in trouble. It's just that you mentioned something about Mikey that surprised us."

Lydia's voice sounded very guarded. I was actually afraid we were about to lose her now. I waved my arms to get Mary's attention to smooth things over.

I shouldn't have worried. Mary was an expert at this.

"It's just that I know Mikey's been going through a hard time. And I wanna make sure you're safe. And that's the truth."

"I'm fine." There was no mistaking the hardness in Lydia's tone now. I winced. Now she was defensive.

"I know," Mary said, her voice super soft as she tried to smooth things over. "But you're pregnant, so I just wanna look out for you."

"You don't need to worry about me in regards to Mikey. If I hadn't met him, I don't know what I would do. The guy doesn't drink or do drugs. He holds a job and is respectful. That's a heck of a lot more than most of the men I've met. It's other relatives you should be worried about."

"I'm sorry," Mary said again. "I didn't mean to offend you."

"Don't bother calling me again. I don't want your clothes." And with that the phone snapped off.

We all stared at the phone for a second, probably all of us feeling disturbed by how the call went. Mary put it in perfect words. "Well, that's not what I thought would go down."

"Me neither," I said.

"No matter what it's obvious she likes Mikey." Lucy nodded.

"She's being loyal to him," I agreed.

"I wonder what she meant about his other relatives?" Lucy asked.

"Especially since it was Mikey who was a wild child."

I looked at my doodle on the paper. I had drawn a man. One with a Richie-Rich swirl on the top of his head. I wondered if we needed to look into Christopher again. "What about Christopher?"

Mary raised a skeptical eyebrow. "You know he's a saint."

"But what if he did stand to inherit Mr. Dee's Estate?"

"Mr. Dee said that he would change his will only if Mikey didn't change or shape up. And, by Lydia's account just now, it certainly sounds like he did."

I shook my head. "Actually, that's not true. We were told he might do it if Mikey didn't shape up. But what if he amended his will anyway?"

It wasn't a great question, but it's the one we had to end our night on. Morning came early around here, I swear sooner than other places. We had a full day of work to look forward to tomorrow.

CHAPTER TWENTY-ONE

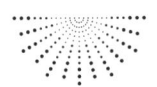

*A*fter lunch, we girls found ourselves in the butler's pantry, polishing the silverware. It was an odd job and I sort of hated it. I also liked it because it was soothing and satisfying to see the utensils gleam.

My phone rang. I glanced at the number and made a face before handing it to Mary.

"Who is it?" she asked, setting down her polishing cloth.

"Just the guy you made a date with on my phone."

"He's actually calling? He didn't get a clue from me not showing up? What a loser." She stared at the phone for a second as it rattled in her hand like a baby rattlesnake. Sighing, she answered it. "Hello?"

Of course, I only got the conversation from her side. "Oh, I'm not there? I guess I'm late, then, baby."

A long pause, and then, "Am I coming? You can't catch my vibe? Let me tell you I don't like cheaters. Who did you cheat on? Think about it for a minute. If you find a woman who thinks you're anything but the chump you really are, you should really hang on to her. Maybe spoil her and keep her convinced never to leave you, because otherwise you have no chance."

She hung up just in the nick of time. The back door opened and Stephen and Thomas came through. Both men were sweaty in the way that spoke of hard physical work and was actually quite attractive. I noticed Mary's smile gauge up a hundred percent.

"Hi, boys. You here for lunch?" She included Stephen but had eyes only for Thomas.

The young man wiped his dark hair from his eyes. "Just looking to wash up."

"I'll get you a fresh towel," she said.

He followed her, but kept a further following distance than she liked. "Well, come on," she encouraged.

As they left, Stephen walked over and we grinned. "I feel like I'm watching two kids go off to their first dance."

"I'd say one is a little unwilling." I worked on a spoon.

He laughed. "I think he's afraid Mary will eat him up."

"He'd do well to heed that worry," I said and we cracked up.

The two returned and Thomas and Stephen started for the kitchen for their lunch.

"Bye, Thomas." Mary waggled her fingers.

Thomas ducked his head with a quiet "bye" and practically ran through the door to make his escape.

"He's so cute," Mary sighed.

"You keep flirting with Thomas, but he's not biting," I said. Maybe I was poking the bear. I guess I'd find out by her reaction.

"He just doesn't know me yet. He's shy."

"Are you sure about that?" I grinned.

"I wonder if he has a brother," Lucy said.

The sibling question made me curious. "Mary, do you have any sisters?" I asked.

"Only brothers," Mary answered. "You?"

"I'm an only. A lonely only. I always wished I had siblings. Maybe somebody younger to pick on."

"I can't see you picking on anyone," Mary grabbed a fork. "You're too nice."

"You know who hasn't been very nice lately,? Miss Janice, that's who," Lucy said.

I shrugged. "I think this all has been hard on her."

Mary nodded as she set the fork down and grabbed another.

"She's lonely," I added.

"Especially after the last guy," Lucy said emphatically. We all made agreement grunts.

"I wonder if her ad ever paid out," I mused.

"Her what? An ad?" both girls said in stereo.

"Have you been holding out on us?" Mary asked.

I blushed. Miss Janice would probably kill me if she knew I was gonna share this. But these girls would never tell. "That's how she found out about the threat. She was reading the personal ads. I guess she put one in herself."

"You're kidding me." Mary groaned.

Lucy looked afraid. "Are you serious? Doesn't she know how dangerous that is?"

"Maybe at some point in your life you realize danger is worth living for," Mary said.

"I think she feels like she got more than she bargained for with Mr. Dee's death."

Mary reached for a butter knife. "We need to figure that out. What do we know about Christopher?"

"We know he hates Tommy the old foreman. And he came to rescue Mr. Dee," I said.

"How about the time he landed the helicopter in the center of the city park to drop off the donation? That's a big deal," Mary added.

I made a face. "Kind of an attention grabber."

"You think so?" She laid the sarcasm thick. "And then there's this crazy will."

"What's all this malarkey I hear in here?" Miss Janice appeared among us out of nowhere. We all flinched as though a wasp buzzed us while we ate watermelon. Lucy's eyes rounded like a deer in the headlights.

"Hi, Miss Janice," I began.

She interrupted me. "What's all this about a will?"

Her question horrified me to realize how much she had heard. When I still didn't answer she put her hands on her thin hips. "I heard you guys discussing Mr. Dee's will. What's going on?"

"We were trying to figure out who might be the beneficiary," Lucy stammered.

"I hope you're not meddling."

I swallowed hard and then decided just to be honest. "Maybe a little," I said. "We're trying to figure out who might have benefited from his death."

"You mean Mikey?"

"We heard that Mikey and Mr. Dee had a falling out."

Her thickly mascaraed eyes narrowed. "So he did have a reason when he came over here all upset that we were gossiping about him, hm?"

My finger immediately went to a hangnail on my thumb, and I wanted to bite it. Instead I clenched my hand into a fist and waited.

She spun around to look at the other girls. "No one else going to answer me? Cat got your tongue?"

At that moment I saw Hank disappear through the crack in the wainscoting from where he'd been sitting in the sunshine. The irony was thick.

Lucy hesitantly started, "I knew someone who worked there and thought I could ask how things were going."

"I see. Just being all neighborly, huh?" When none of us responded, she shook her head and continued with her caustic bite. "Why didn't you come to me?"

Of course, none of us answered.

"At any rate, I'm good friends with Mr. Merryweather. He's their family attorney who'll be sharing the will. He did the estate for my dear husband when he passed. He was the executor." She touched her chin thoughtfully. "I think if I invite him over for dinner—a little laughter, a little wine—he'd be willing to let it slip. I'll go get Marguerite now. In the meantime you ladies stay out of trouble."

CHAPTER TWENTY-TWO

We met up later in the laundry room.

"I'm telling you, I have a good feeling about this theory," Mary said, in excitement. "What if everyone knows that Mikey wore that red plaid jacket?"

"Your asking if the person at the bar was—"

We said it together in the way that showed that kinship between close friends. "Christopher."

"He's about the same size as Mikey. I think he could wear his jacket."

"Should we go back to the bartender with a picture to see if he can identify Mikey?" I suggested.

Mary took the other ends of the sheet and shook it out. The material was still warm from the iron and smelled like the lilac spray.

"I think Larry won't be very helpful, especially since I kind of burned that bridge already." Mary gave that evil grin of hers. "It was worth it. But remember he thought you were sitting with the Emerald girls."

"Yeah?"

"I happen to know which girls he's referring to. It's a birthday club, and they go out for everybody's birthday to celebrate and have fun."

"Great. How do we get a hold of them?"

"My brother's wife's mom is one of those Emerald Girls. She works at the local pet groomers. I say we run another errand night."

We both looked at Hank lying on the bed.

"Hank, sweetie," I wheedled. "You want to get groomed?"

Mary squinted her eyes. "He probably needs some kind of bug protection at the very least."

"A flea bath?"

Hank opened his eyes like two green laser beams. His tail lashed.

Mary must have thought she went too far, because she softened her stance. "Maybe just a good brushing. It's the gossip we're there for. Let me run it by Marguerite and have her ask Miss Janice. I'm sure at the mention of fleas she'll be more than happy to let us go."

I remember how I'd found Hank snuggled in a pile of blankets on Miss Janice's bed and figured we'd have our answer within five minutes of Marguerite's request.

It was three minutes. Marguerite told us where the cat kennel was located, and we bundled him up. Less than an hour from the start of our conversation, we arrived at the pet groomers with a very unhappy Hank.

It was a cute little boutique with the large front window stuffed with a display of doggy coats and stuffed animals. A soapy white bathtub had been painted on the center of the window with bubbles surrounding happy dogs with their pink tongues poking out.

Mary turned off the car, and I wrapped my arms around the wiggling box. Hank gave a pitiful meow. I blew kisses through the holes to try to comfort him. I really didn't want any part of this, because I knew Hank would be mad at me, but Mary insisted that I come along.

We walked inside the boutique, and a bird whistle over the door announced our arrival. Clouds of fuzzy white hair floated through the air, and I immediately wanted to sneeze. A large white dog was being bathed in the sink.

The woman bathing him wore a rubber apron and had suds clear up to her elbows. The dog panted with a happy smile and actually did look an awful lot like the painting on the window. Obviously he enjoyed the warm water and the massage.

"I'll be with you in a minute," the woman called above the sound of the spray.

"That's her. That's Alice," Mary whispered to me.

I checked out the place. We were alone, however there was no place to sit, so we stood by the door. Behind the counter another technician had a dachshund on the table and was carefully clipping his nails. A long shelf next to me held just about every kind of dog food I'd ever heard of, along with dog treats, shampoos, toys, dog jackets, and I swear what looked like tiny rain boots.

The bird whistled again as a young woman came in. The helper doing the nails glanced up and smiled. "He's done now. He's been such a good boy!" The pup was lifted off the table and given a treat while the two women chatted. The owner completed her payment and carried the dachshund out.

Alice finished the dog bath. She carefully shut a shower curtain around the tub so the dog could shake. And shake he did, with his tail thumping against the plastic bin like a drum beat.

Alice called to the young woman. "Jeffrey is ready now. Can you please take him for his little blow dry?"

She passed over the leash to her helper and washed her hands. Finally, she walked over to us. "How can I help you?"

"Blow dry?" I asked with a smile. The word conjured up a picture of a pink hair bag and curlers.

"We have a machine that blows warm air, and the dogs just love it. They can walk around and shake. After that they get their grooming."

From inside the box, Hank gave a long meow.

"Oh, you have a cat?" she asked and leaned over the counter to look.

"We wonder if you offer a cat bath for fleas," I said, feeling like Judas.

She walked over to the shelf and pulled out the shampoo. After a moment, she grabbed a second bottle. "You can't put just anything on cats. Make sure it's formulated for their metabolism. This is gentle and organic. But not all cats like baths, as I'm sure you already know." She peered inside the kennel. "Does he have matted fur or knots?"

I shook my head. "No. He keeps himself very well-groomed."

Alice passed over the second bottle. "In that case, I suggest spritzing a bit of this one on his brush and giving him a once-over. He'll enjoy that and it won't disrupt his PH balance."

I accepted the spray, happy to hear we could forgo the bath. I wandered over to the shelf. From its stuffed offerings, I chose a brush and, a second later, picked up a little mouse filled with catnip.

Mary waited by the counter. "So I think I saw you last week at the Purple Pig."

The woman laughed. "Oh, yes. We went there for a girls' gathering we like to do now and then."

"I don't know if you remember me, but I'm Samuel's sister."

"Ah! Samuel, my favorite son-in-law. How are you?"

"I'm doing well. So did you notice the fight that happened at the bar that night?"

"I sure did," Alice answered. "Between those two guys. And one stormed off."

I found Mikey's picture on social media and showed it to her. "Was it him?"

She took the phone from me and studied it. "I'm not sure. I thought the guy seemed thinner. Although I really only saw the back of him. All I really remember was his red plaid jacket." She handed it back.

"Do you remember what they were fighting about?"

"Something about mining. Or wills? I'm not sure."

My ears pricked at the mention of mining. "I heard he had a hard time driving the jeep out. Did you notice?"

Alice laughed. "No, by that point I was having too much fun with my friends."

We thanked her and headed out.

I put Hank in the back seat and scooted next to him. "I know you're mad. But, without you, we might not have learned the information we needed. You are a hero, Hank."

Hank stared at me with angry eyes from the back of the kennel.

"I was a jerk, and I know it." I took the toy and shook it until the little bell rang. Hank ignored it. I made the mouse's tail wiggle in front of him, trying to entice him. He blinked green eyes, bored.

Sighing, I climbed into the passenger seat. "So she didn't recognize Mikey. That's interesting."

"I'm not sure. He has lost a bit of weight recently. Maybe he looks different than that picture." She sighed.

I snapped on my seatbelt. "Well, at least Alice was nice. And she likes your brother. She said he was her favorite son-in-law."

Mary chuckled. "He's her only son-in-law."

CHAPTER TWENTY-THREE

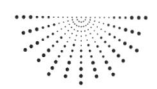

We returned home to discover that Miss Janice had scheduled her dinner plans for this very evening. Cook made her famous Beef Wellington along with garlic potatoes and bacon-wrapped asparagus. She topped everything off with a cherry pie that had a beautiful flaky crust and oozed syrup.

All of which were Mr. Merryweather's favorites. Marguerite had the good wine chilling. I was told to make sure the humidor in the cigar room carried Mr. Merryweather's favorite brand and then to dress in my whites.

He arrived at seven on the dot. Butler took his overcoat and showed him into the parlor where Marguerite waited with a snifter of brandy. From there Miss Janice led him to the family dining room, a cozier version of the formal, still bright with its hand-cut chandelier and Baccarat candle holders. I came through with the crystal water pitcher and filled the glasses while Marguerite topped his wine glass.

When we brought out the first course (small vessels of lobster bisque) Mr. Merryweather was already on his second glass of wine and appeared to be relishing the company. Conversation swirled around topics that had Miss Janice's cheeks pink from amusement.

I cleared the first course. Lucy stopped me by the sink. "Guess what, I got a text!"

"What does it say?"

"Well," Lucy grinned like she knew she had a prize. "It says my boyfriend wants me back."

I rolled my eyes hard, letting her know that if she gave in to him I'd never let her live it down.

"You better not," I cautioned.

She giggled. "This is after Mary's dressing down. I guess it worked."

"Mary is everyone's bulldog," I said. "I don't ever wanna be on her bad side."

The rest of dinner went off without a hitch. I never heard Miss Janice pop the question about the will, but when I brought out the pie, she winked at me. She was on her second glass of wine as well.

They retired to the cigar room for a final drink, which left us to clear the table.

The next morning the news came through Marguerite as we drank our morning coffee and prepared for the day.

"You're hardly gonna believe this," she said, "But Mikey is not inheriting the bulk of the will."

I gasped while Cook choked on her coffee. "That scoundrel," she announced.

"Cook! That's not nice to speak ill of the dead."

Cook mumbled she was sorry but her lowered eyebrows contradicted the apology. I understood. Cutting his son out of the will was very cold.

"Who is it, then?" I asked.

"Christopher."

"I knew it!" Mary said, jerking her head up from her phone.

"So what do we do now? Call the police?"

"They're professional. They already knew this and they're still looking into Miss Janice."

"I wish we'd showed Alice a picture of Christopher."

"We can go back, I guess. She did say she only saw the back of him. I'm not sure it would help."

"There was that mining Alice mentioned." I let the thought hang in the air like a fishing line, hoping to hook Mary.

It did.

"This Wednesday is our day off," she added.

"See you then."

CHAPTER TWENTY-FOUR

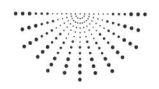

That Wednesday, I patted the statue for good luck. My gut feeling told me I would need it today.

"Are we really going to do this?" I asked, as I met Mary at the bottom of the stairs.

"I feel like that's the missing key somehow," she answered while tying her shoe.

"Second time's the charm, huh?"

"Let's do this!" I grabbed two water bottles, remembering last time, and we headed outside. I wished we could have borrowed Stephen's lawn mower, because the walk seemed daunting, especially at the pace Mary was taking. With her chin down, arms thrusting forward, she pushed through the field grass like we were on a race.

However, it did seem like we arrived quicker this time. Maybe because we knew our way. Experience.

The old buildings were just as dark and scary as the first time I'd seen it. I wasn't too eager to search through the structures.

Mary approached the little building first and walked up the steps. She paused as one cracked. It settled a few inches lower but held. "I don't think we'll fall through," she decided.

I wasn't exactly bolstered by her vote of confidence, but I followed behind. She tried the door with its wooden door handle. It didn't budge. Lips pressed in determination, she put her hips behind it and shoved the door. It opened with creaks and shudders, but she at least succeeded.

The interior was like nothing I'd seen before. Like a time capsule, the room contained old chairs, a table, even a bed. Above us, the ceiling bowed inward in an alarming way. The afternoon sunlight splashed through the doorway across the floor and against the farthest wall. It highlighted how many dust fairies filled the air. I pulled my shirt up to cover my nose.

"What are you doing?" she asked.

"This dust is crazy." I gestured to the floating particles.

"I'd be more scared of that." She pointed to a centipede the size of a silver dollar that slithered inside a crack in the floorboard.

"That's disgusting." I winced, backing up.

"Is this where the boy was found? Some closet?"

Carefully, I walked along the floor, flinching at the creaking boards. I found a closet, but it seemed solid, no false barrier. I tried knocking on all the walls. I felt pretty sure there was nothing new here that the police didn't see the first time. I even peeked into the crack in the floor that our multi-legged friend disappeared into.

"Let's check the other building," Mary suggested.

"The boy said the treasure was under here," I said.

Mary nodded but still cautiously made her way out.

The church stairs were in better shape, however the interior was sad. All the pews now lay on their sides. Something had come through and pushed everything around. Even the podium had been knocked over.

Mary moved around the litter. The flashlight beam from her cell phone jolted with each step across the rough floor like an odd little mouse. The light jumped over piles of debris and over the benches. I stood in the center of the room for a minute, and tried to take it all in. What was it about this place that made it so valuable? If there was gold, where was it?

Aimlessly I walked from one side of the room to the other, listening closely to my steps to detect if I could hear any hollow spaces. Whoever built this did a good job, because the floor felt solid under my feet.

Upfront, the podium lay toppled over like a toy soldier some child had forgotten about. I walked around a bench and picked up a Bible from the floor. There was no doubt it was old and dusty, but I swear I saw one just like it at my grandma's house.

I opened the Bible to the copyright and read the date, 1945. I was surprised. So old but not as old as this building. Someone else had come in here at one point. Perhaps to worship or take a quiet moment to pray.

"Oh my gosh!" Mary shouted in excitement.

"What did you find?" I asked, trying to hurry over to her. My feet got entangled around the bars of a chair that had been turned upside down.

"I can't believe the police left it like this." And then she held up a pen.

"The bible is kind of modern, too." I set it gently on a pew.

Then I walked over to the podium. I couldn't stand to see it tipped over any longer. Maybe this one thing I could fix. I tipped it up. I knew right where it should be. There was a square on the floor where the wood was a lighter color. I tipped the heavy piece back and forth to "walk" it to the spot. I was nearly there when I heard a funny creak.

Because of all the creaks similarly sounding that I've heard, having now lived in the Thornberry house—with its hidden tunnels—I immediately became alert.

"Mary, did you hear that?"

"I sure did." Mary came over. Together we lifted the podium and moved it back, so we could examine the pale square. She gingerly tested each of the planks with her foot. On one of the tries, the other end of the board sprang up with a crack. We grinned at each other with excitement, and she bent over and tried to pry it up. Other than lifting a half an inch, it remained firmly in place.

"Try it again," I suggested.

She walked over to the original spot that made the first creaking noise. This time we focused on the floor by tapping the length of it.

"Go over to where the podium was supposed to be and stand in that spot," Mary said.

I walked over to the yellow square and started poking at those boards. Mary remained on the board that she'd popped up. When I stood in the center of the square, both boards popped up.

After the initial surprise, we pried them up together. The boards opened to reveal a primitive switch. When we pressed the switch, a four foot section of the floor opened up.

I stared at Mary, and she gave me the same wide-eyed expression until we both gave into uncontrollably giggles.

"We did it! We did it!" I shouted.

CHAPTER TWENTY-FIVE

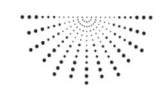

We stared down the dark shaft. The top was bottlenecked with swaying cobwebs.

"Bring me a light," I said.

Mary scrambled for her phone, nearly dropping it down the hole in her eagerness. She flashed the light through the opening.

We both leaned in to peer into the dark abyss. I wasn't sure how deep it would be. In fact, I was half-afraid it would turn out to be the well I'd heard about. Then I saw the remaining afternoon light wash down the dirt surfaces along the sides.

"I see the bottom," Mary said, confidently.

"This is it." I grinned at Mary. "This is what that boy found. I'm sure of it."

"There is no way that little kid moved the podium and, coincidentally, two people stepped on the boards on opposite sides and then picked up the trap door," Mary said sarcastically.

"No, but look." I pointed to one end of the cavern. "That tunnel there connects somewhere out back."

"Do you want to do this? Are we going to pretend this isn't as creepy as it is?"

I glanced down at the hole again, trying to weigh the feasibility. "I think if we lean over the edge and let our legs dangle, we can get to the bottom with just a little jump." I gestured to her phone. "How much battery do you have?"

She checked. "About twenty-three percent." I made a face and she grinned sheepishly. "I forgot to charge it. I was stuck in the laundry yesterday, so that means a lot of YouTube videos."

"I guess we could go back for a flashlight."

"I don't think we have time to go back."

With that, she rolled over to dangle her legs over the ledge.

"Are we doing this? We're doing this." I said as she dropped down.

Her voice sounded far away. "Hurry!"

She left me no choice but to follow her. I went over the same way and landed with a jolt.

Slowly, I straightened my knees. They hurt. I hobbled forward to shake off the stiffness.

Mary moved her flashlight around. The walls were rough with rocks poking through the hard-packed dirt. The tunnel did appear to lead straight back to the shack we'd just come from.

"It definitely connects the two places," Mary announced. We followed the dirt track, our sneakers scarcely making a sound on the soft dusty floor. I kept a careful eye out for rodents and spiders, but I couldn't stop my smile from the thrill of our discovery.

The light hit something ahead of us.

"What's this?" Mary asked. Her beam sparkled on a chunk of metal attached to the wall. Carefully, she brought it down. "It's a badge. How interesting. And look at this." She pointed to a wooden box. Inside were two bottles. There was an empty space for a third.

"Someone recently took one," she said, the light shaking in her hand as she excitedly shined it around.

"How could you possibly tell?" I asked.

"Look at the dust. It's thick everywhere but that empty spot." She pointed the light in. "Look, there's liquid in there. It's probably ancient."

She leaned over to grab it. I immediately yelled, "Don't touch it."

"Come on. Let's just take a peek," she said.

"The bottle might have fingerprints on it," I answered.

"Fingerprints?"

"I just don't know, but I have a feeling."

"Your gut feeling?"

I nodded. She knew me well enough to know sometimes my gut knew things I didn't even understand. She left the crate alone and starting texting.

I didn't have to ask because she went on to explain. "I'm letting Stephen know where we are in case we need some help."

"Good thinking," I said.

We continued on. The tunnel opened to a little room. Inside was a stack of shovels and a pick. A little chair and a metal safe were next to the tools.

The safe door had been left open on sprung hinges. Mary flashed the light inside.

There was a paper rectangle shape, ancient and yellow.

"Maybe we should leave it," I said. "It might disintegrate."

She shined the light over it. "It's written in some other language."

"Take a picture," I suggested.

"Good idea!" She snapped a shot. She rubbed the screen with her thumb, trying to zoom in. "Blackstone. Does this mean what I think it does?"

"A deed? I'm not sure. We need to go back and find out."

She grimaced. "Probably should hurry. I'm down to four-percent battery."

"Great news. So do we continue on to find the closet where the boy was found? Or try and have you climb on my shoulders to get out the other hole?"

She took a deep breath. "Two percent. Let's go forward fast. I'm starting to freak out."

CHAPTER TWENTY-SIX

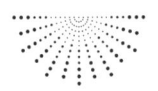

We hurried down the path. Neither of us talked now. I think we both were running on frayed nerves. Images of being stuck down here played in my mind, and I think hers as well. I was also incredibly thankful that she'd contacted Stephen for a back-up plan.

"Is that what I think it is?" Mary asked.

I peered around her and could see nothing. "What?"

Just then, the light on the phone went out. Mary whimpered. I couldn't make a sound since the air in my lungs disappeared at the same time as the light.

Then I saw what she was referring to. A dim line broke the darkness ahead.

"Keep going," I said.

We moved forward. My hands were out to protect my face, however, at the same time I was terrified they would touch something. And by something, I meant wiggly legs.

The line grew brighter as we approached. A few more steps and we could see it was a crack between boards.

"Push it," I encouraged her.

She shoved at it, but nothing happened. I pressed the board with all my weight along with her. With a loud crack, the board broke and we tumbled into a room. I sat up and glanced around.

Chairs, a bed. We had made it back into the shack.

I remembered the centipede and hurried to my feet.

"Well, that was a lovely adventure," Mary said dryly, brushing herself off. We made the journey outside as swiftly as the creaking floor would allow. I couldn't get out of here fast enough.

We staggered down the creaking porch like two drunkards as the unstable stairs sagged under our feet.

"That was fun," I said, back on stable ground.

"Fun until the phone died," Mary added.

I laughed. "At least our lives aren't boring. Now what we have to do is to talk about the common denominator."

"What, now you're talking math to me?"

"No, I'm saying what do we do about Christopher? Do we call the police now?"

"And tell them what? We discovered a tunnel?" She picked a cobweb off her shirt.

"We found the Blackstone name in the photo," I reminded her.

"I think we should get that book from the library. You know, the one that proves the link to Mr. Dee's bloodline."

We started back. I pushed through the tall grass, not fearing the bugs now. They had no power over me after seeing that centipede.. Still I somehow carried the chill of that underground tunnel despite the hot sun.

"I keep going back to Christopher. How do you think he makes money?" I stubbornly continued.

"Just doing what rich people do, I guess."

"Marguerite said Mr. Dee had fallen on to hard times, no chauffeur. You think Christopher just mooched off of him?"

"No. He was known for his philanthropy work. Cook said so." She groaned. "Dang we forgot our water."

"We're almost back. So Mr. Dee hit hard times, but it doesn't seem like Christopher has. Did he bail Mr. Dee out? I'm so curious what he does for money. After all, Mikey was working in car sales not too long ago."

"He once studied to be a nurse, right?" Mary wiped at her face, leaving a dirt streak.

"True. He's not one now."

The manor stood tall before us. I could have kissed it right on its lion nose knocker.

"Yeah, but he went to Mr. Dee's manor to help out or something like that. Let's go see if Cook has any answers. She always seems to have the inside scoop."

We stumbled into the kitchen, where we both raced for drinks of water. Cook watched us with arched eyebrows. She remained silent as she peeled apples alongside Jessie, who was mixing dough.

"What are you making?" I finally asked, as I wiped water from my mouth.

"Apple streusel cake," Cook said. "Miss Janice is having a tea party. Today was to be a girls' luncheon, but she canceled it." Cook widened her eyes as if to say, "You know what happened."

"Because of..." Mary let the sentence hang.

"Gossip moves faster in this town than a pat of butter on a hot cob of corn. And all of the women canceled the luncheon except for Mrs. Fitzwater."

My heart squeezed with appreciation. Mrs. Fitzwater was truly the kind of person you want in your corner.

"So it's just her then?" Lucy asked.

"Just her. So I am determined to make this the best lunch ever." Cook's lips pressed together firmly as her hands flashed slicing apples. "Maybe we'll set it out in the rose garden. Stephen's opened it back up. It's been overgrown for so long. That's where Mr. Thornberry proposed to Miss Janice years ago. Did you know they planted five white roses to symbolize the fifth of June. That's the day he proposed to her. I think they'd hoped their children would marry there as well."

"But they had no children," Mary said.

Marguerite came in, her hands full with an expensive china tea set that I'd never seen before.

"What are you ladies doing in here? Bored? I'll have you using that energy to wash all the windows in the west wing."

"We wanted to ask Cook if she knew what Christopher did for a living."

Marguerite's forehead rumpled. "Doesn't he live on his inheritance from his parents?"

"Oh," I said. "They died?"

"About ten years ago or so." Marguerite put her finger on her chin before looking at Cook. "Do you remember that?"

"Somewhere around then," Cook answered as she liberally sprinkled cinnamon.

"Is that why he lives with Mr. Dee?"

"I think he moved in when Mr. Dee needed help."

"You mean when he got sick?" I asked.

Marguerite shook her head, her gray curls wobbling. "No. Mikey got into some trouble. I think Mr. Dee invited Christopher to come help sort Mikey out."

I thought about Mikey's old car salesman boss I'd talked to and wondered if that was the trouble.

"Was it a couple of years ago?" I asked.

"That seems about right," Marguerite said.

"Did you know Christopher before then?" Mary asked. She'd finished fanning herself down and now looked for something in the cookie jar.

"Christopher and his family were not there at the manor much," Cook said.

"To be honest, I'd only heard of them in passing," Marguerite said.

"I remember Christopher coming up as a little boy." Cook threw a smug look at Marguerite. She, of course, loved the opportunity to rub in that she had been here longer than the head housekeeper. "He was a shy little boy. And his parents were terribly thin and uptight. They never let him play outside. Never let him have so much as a popsicle.

Christopher grew up to be a bit of a tattletale, so that caused a little bit of a rivalry between Mikey and him."

Jessie leaned against the counter with her phone out. "Well, this is weird."

I knew she wasn't going to answer unless I asked. "What?"

"Get this, Christopher received a degree in chemistry in college."

"How on earth did you find that out?" I leaned forward. In the back of my mind I had a new worry. Were college classes public knowledge? Would everyone know I'd taken water aerobics my freshman year?"

"It's in his bio on his business link. Along with a slew of other accomplishments. Also, his last name is different."

Mary twinned her head next to Jessie's. "That's incredible, Jessie! What a find!"

"I'm missing something," I confessed. "It's different than Mr. Dee's?"

Cook shrugged. "I already knew that. It's not hard to explain. It's Mr. Dee's cousin, but they're not blood-related. His great grandma married into the family."

"Okay." I hate trying to figure out cousins and distant relatives. Twice removed, whatever.

"So here's the kicker. Christopher's great Grandma was the original Blackstone."

My mouth dropped. "You're kidding me? We need to get that book again."

"Tonight at book club," Marguerite promised. "We'll finish our talk then."

CHAPTER TWENTY-SEVEN

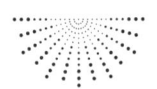

*L*ater that night, Mary knocked on my bedroom door. "You ready?"

"Yeah, let's go." Dressed in my pj's, hair in a scrunchy, I followed Mary down to Marguerite's room. On the way, Mary whispered, "That Christopher, man. He's a mystery. Black sheep vs white sheep kind of thing."

"So, he's the white sheep?"

"Yeah. Sure. The goodie-two-shoes." She bit her lip. "Do you think he likes me?"

"Who, Christopher?"

"Thomas! The new gardener!"

I felt like I'd experienced conversation whiplash. "I guess? He hasn't really had a chance to get to know you."

She sighed. "He didn't even look in my direction at breakfast today. Didn't you notice?"

I frowned. I could barely remember what I'd eaten, let alone who looked at who. "He probably was a little overwhelmed. We're a loud crowd."

I could smell the popcorn wafting down the hallway before we even arrived at Marguerite's room. It made me wonder how long we could keep the room a secret if we had such tantalizing food each time.

I peeked down the long hallway, but no one was coming. We snuck inside, and Mary shut the door quietly behind us.

The secret club doorway had not been quite pulled closed and the light flickered out of the crack. Mary pulled the door the rest of the way open, and we stepped into to a welcoming scented bloom of buttered popcorn and fresh pizza rolls.

"How do you guys always get here before us?" Mary demanded.

"You're not the last ones. We're still waiting on Marguerite. Miss Janice has kept her a long time tonight," Janet said from her spot on the couch.

"Headache tonic?"

"It took two tonight," Janet whipped her thin blonde braid over her shoulder and propped her feet up on the stool. On her lap lay a thick book.

"What's that?" Lucy asked.

"I think we should read this one for our next book." Janet held it up, and I read the title. The Nighttime Circus.

Lucy leaned in. "What's it about?"

Janet read the back. Right in the middle of the description, Marguerite bustled through the door. Her cheeks were pink and her hair curls especially frenzied. "Good gracious, have you started without me?"

"We have indeed," Cook said and popped a pizza roll into her mouth.

Marguerite scowled. "You better have saved some of those for me. I'm the one who put those on the grocery list."

Cook brushed off her hands. "I think that was the last one," she said emphatically.

Marguerite's lips moved as if to give a spicy retort until Lucy interrupted. She pointed to a tray on the table next to one of the bookshelves. "They're right here, Marguerite."

Marguerite glared at Cook. "You always try to poke at me," she snapped.

"But you make it so easy." Cook smiled.

When we all finally had our snacks and were situated, Marguerite strolled to the front of the room.

"I swear, I hardly have the energy to do this tonight," she warned.

Just then Hank poked his head out from the wainscoting and sauntered into the room with all of us cooing. And he knew he was the cutest baby. He minced up to Lucy. She offered him a bite of pizza roll. After taking a careful sniff he backed away, his tail making snake shapes in the air. I held out a piece of popcorn but didn't fare any better. He finally waltzed over to Lucy and hopped up into her lap.

"He chose me," she said with a happy grin.

"Ladies," Marguerite said again, exasperated. "You'd think that cat was running this club."

"He's more exciting than the alternative you're offering us, that's for sure," Cook said. "And he probably wants to know where we are in solving Mr. Dee's murder."

Marguerite glared at her. "You want an update then?"

"And what is that?" Cook asked.

Marguerite waved at Mary, who took over. "We're starting to have suspicions with a new person."

"Christopher?" Cook asked.

"How did you know?" Lucy gaped.

"They were asking about him in the kitchen earlier."

"Yes, that's right. Don't you think he appeared out of the blue into this family? We can't quite figure out why he ended up living with Mr. Dee."

"It was good that he did, because Mr. Dee had the diabetic situation. It led to a stroke."

Mary nodded thoughtfully. "But what about Christopher's own family? And I don't mean his parents," she shot at Marguerite. "For instance, where has he worked? Where did he use to live? Was he ever married?"

Several girls got out their phones and were already doing a search.

"I don't know about his past family, but I heard he got somebody into trouble," Jessie said.

"Into trouble?" I asked. "Isn't that kind of old-fashioned? Pregnancy isn't a disease you know."

"Maybe not, but maybe some people do see it as trouble around here."

"Really? Who was it?" Mary asked.

"It's a rumor that got bantered around the hairdresser's." Jessie answered.

"Mr. Dee's family bloodline is strong," Lucy said.

"What do you mean?" Janet asked.

"I saw Mikey with a pregnant gal not too long ago. I don't think her family liked him though, because they were yelling at him."

"What were they yelling?" Lucy asked.

"They told him to have Christopher call them. That they had done what he asked."

"What did Mikey say to that?" Janet continued.

"Mikey said that was between them and Christopher. He wanted no part of it."

"And then what happened?"

"Then the girl dragged Mikey away and told him that she would talk to him later. She was crying and said thank you over and over again."

"She told Mikey thank you?" I asked.

"Yep. And then that crabby boss of hers grabbed her arm and pulled her back inside that creepy dry cleaning place."

I nudged Mary. "Can I see your phone?"

Her eyebrows wrinkled, but she passed it over. I searched for Lydia's phone number and hit text. I took a deep breath. I knew she didn't want to hear from us again. But I had to try.

Quickly, I texted. **—I'm sorry to bother you, but is Mikey still treating you well?**

I sent it like a Hail Mary, and couldn't have been more shocked to see the three dots showing she was replying back. Soon the response came. **—I wouldn't know what to do without him.**

I dared another text. **—Did Mikey pick you up for your doctor's appointment in his jeep?**

She answered back. **—No. It was his Lincoln. Please don't message me again. I don't want to lose my new job.**

A new job? **—Where did you used to work?**

—I thought you knew. At Mr. Dee's

I sucked in my breath and nudged Mary. She glanced over at the phone. Her eyes widened as she read. Quickly, she snatched it and started typing.

—Did you get fired because you were pregnant?

She sent back a laughing face along with **—You could say that. Ask Christopher. Oh, that's right. He's dumped me.**

Both of us gasped.

CHAPTER TWENTY-EIGHT

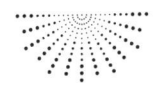

"Look at this!" Mary shouted as she jumped up, running to the front of the room.

"Well, good heavens, what is it?" Marguerite asked, wrinkling her nose and pulling on her glasses. Mary showed her. Marguerite silently read it while Mary watched like a proud parent at a kindergarten teacher meeting.

"I have no idea," Marguerite said when she finished.

Mary rolled her eyes and said in a rush. "This is Lydia. She used to work for Mr. Dee. She's the key!"

"When did she leave?" Jessie asked.

"Probably when the whole lot of employees left. My friend told us Mr. Dee didn't pay her," Janet said.

"She didn't leave. Christopher kicked her out," I reminded everyone of the text.

"What I don't get is if their estate is essentially bankrupt, then why would Mikey want to kill his dad?" Lucy asked.

The candlelight flickered against the bookshelves. The gilded spines glinted, making the mood especially mysterious as we all considered that question.

"Revenge for the will?" Jessie shrugged.

"Mikey didn't know he'd been cut out. After all, he straightened out his life like his dad threatened. They should have been on good terms."

"Who has some paper?" I asked. "We need to get this stuff down." Maybe it was because I was a doodler, but I could think better with a pencil.

Cook fumbled for a pen from her pocket and Lucy slid across a notebook.

"First of all," I began. "Let's talk about the Friday night of the gala. We know that Mikey did not drive his usual vehicle. Lydia says he showed up in the Lincoln. We also have a witness who saw Mikey in his jeep, but driving it poorly. Any guesses as to who that person was?"

"Someone who was imitating Mikey, that's for sure."

I nodded. "There's a slim chance it could be the old foreman, because he had a beef with Mr. Dee as well."

"Who, Tommy?" Cook asked. "That man is the size of a side of beef. No way would he be mistaken for Mikey."

"Then that leaves only one other person. Anyone want to guess?"

"The beneficiary of the will, Christopher!" Mary chimed in proudly. "Which makes sense because he had access to the jacket and knew just what to do to imitate his cousin."

"Okay, then. What witnesses do we have?" I asked, pencil ready. I saw that I'd already drawn a curlicue around my number one.

Janet raised her hand. "I know the answer to this one! There are several. The women's birthday club, the bartender, and the waitress at the steak house."

"We need to get Christopher's picture in front of them," I said. "Any ideas how?"

"We kind of burned the bridge to Larry," Mary said with a guilty look.

Lucy laughed. "Not necessarily, he did just message me."

"Did you write him back?" Mary's eyes narrowed.

Lucy blushed and nodded.

"I don't know whether to be mad at you or kiss you for responding to him. Someone find her a photo of Christopher."

"Give me a sec." Jessie searched on her phone.

"I have a question," Janet said. "Even if it was Christopher, how does Mr. Dee's death benefit him if the estate is bankrupt?"

"I have a picture!" Jessie smiled triumphantly. After a bit of sharing, Lucy was able so send the photo to her ex-boyfriend.

"I'll see if I can get one to Alice," Mary said. "Anyone want to take on the waitress?"

"Let's start with those two. We'll find out soon enough. And then we'll call the police," Marguerite said.

Cook lifted a shoulder. "You might be surprised ladies. They might already be on top of this."

"Who knows. They did check into our Miss Janice. At any rate, it's getting late now. Let me remind you, tomorrow starts our deep cleaning. Let's get to bed and have a fresh start in the morning."

We all got up to leave. Cook took one last cookie. Mary met me at the door with the historical book tucked under her arm.

"Check it out tonight and let me know what you think," she whispered. "I expect a book report in the morning." She grinned.

"Really, a book report, and deep cleaning early in the morning?"

"You're a professional. You can handle it," she teased, as we split in different directions to go to our rooms.

CHAPTER TWENTY-NINE

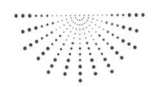

I set the book on the dresser and crawled into bed. At first, I stared at the ceiling, thinking about the tunnel, Lydia, and now Christopher. I couldn't sleep. How was I supposed to with all this information spinning in my head? I rolled over to see the time, and my gaze ended up on a picture of my mom and grandma and me.

I felt a bittersweet squeeze at the sight of mom's face. I was going to see them next weekend and I couldn't wait. It would be nice to let all of this craziness go and get back to something more normal. Maybe mom would have her chicken and dumplings for dinner. That was my favorite comfort food of all time. A big bowl of it on grandma's TV trays that she still used for movie night, in front of a Hallmark movie. Grandma would tell us what was about to happen next, because she had seen them all a hundred times.

Mom would shake her head and say, "Not again, ma!" And I'd laugh.

I needed to see them. Grinning at the memory, I laid back and wiggled my feet.

Hey, where was Hank? I sat up and stared at the cupboard door that remained tightly closed, showing no signs of any intruding kitty paw.

Sleep was impossible now. Sighing, I resigned myself to a little insomnia and shrugged on my robe. I picked up the book Mary had borrowed from the secret library, then headed to the study.

Downstairs, I flipped on the lamp and found Hank already sleeping on his cushion by Mr. Thornberry's desk. He lifted his head and gave me a soft welcome mew.

"Hey, buddy," I said and bent to rub his cheek.

The hush of the room was as comforting to me as one of my grandma's old quilts, the one she'd made from grandpa's worn flannel shirts. I sat in a chair, tucked my feet under myself, and opened the book to the contents. History had always fascinated me. But tonight impatience dampened that normal zing of interest.

Moments later, I heard soft pads and then Hank jumped next to me. He sniffed my face before sitting down and licking the side of my hand with his rough tongue.

Then he started adjusting to lay down, making me scoot over. Amazing how he could squeeze me out.

I found the chapter Cook had showed us a few days earlier. I studied the picture. Those men. And then I saw something that interested me.

Two men sitting at a table. One held a blank deed. One held a pen. There were no signatures yet, but I was sure that was the same paper I'd seen in the safe.

The blurb talked of gold being found in the area. The deed was to give Mr. Blackstone ownership of the land in five years in recompense for mining tools and chemicals to be used.

Hank rested his paw on the page, right in the middle of what I was reading.

"Hank, can you move, please?"

Apparently the answer was no, so I nudged his paw away. Under it was a paragraph to describe the process of getting gold out of sediment like this, and it involved using mercury and ester. The two mixed together caused a type of reaction that helped separate the gold flakes from the rock.

I read the word again and then grabbed my phone. Quickly, I did a search for the chemical ester. The first thing that came up was a toxicity warning. It was no longer used because of the high mortality rate, caused by hemorrhage.

The victims accidentally contaminated the food they ate after they came into physical contact with it.

As I scrolled through the links, the baby hairs on my neck prickled. The search also pulled up images of the bottle.

It was the same one I'd seen down in the tunnel below the church. And I remembered the empty space where another bottle had been in the wooden carton. Mary had wanted to examine one of the remaining bottles, but I'd stopped her because I was worried about fingerprints.

I jumped up, startling Hank. Clutching the book, I ran out of the study and up the cold stairs. I was out of breath by the time I got to Mary's door. I knocked hard and then leaned against the frame to catch my breath.

She yanked open the door with her hair sticking up like Hank's when I woke him from deep sleep. "What's the emergency?"

I pushed inside. "Remember the bottles we found in the tunnel? It causes death by hemorrhage."

Her jaw dropped. "Like how Mr Dee died?" She sat hard on her bed.

I nodded. "And get this. Remember the paper we saw in the safe? It's the same one as in the photo. Look here." I shoved the book at her. "It's the same one the man is holding. It was their contract. It gave the Blackstones the land in a trade."

We heard pounding footsteps and then a frantic knock on the door.

Mary stood up with an ironic eye roll. "My room is Grand Central Station, apparently."

This time, Lucy stood there breathlessly. "Larry wrote me back about the picture! It's him! It was Christopher in the red jacket at the bar."

Down the hallway, Cook's door slammed open. "What on earth is all the ruckus?" She came out, her pink slippers scuffling on the floor.

"I think we need another meeting," Mary said.

Cooks gaze shifted between us, and she threw up her hands in defeat. "Let's head to the kitchen. I'm feeling like I need a bite to eat, now that Marguerite hogged all the pizza rolls."

"I did what?" grumpily retorted Marguerite, who seemed to appear out of nowhere.

My eyes popped. I'd never seen her in her jammies before. She wore a colorful muumuu with a matching headscarf. I swear I even saw a curler or two.

"I think we figured out who the murderer is," I said.

"Well, don't just stand there. Lead the way." Marguerite bustled ahead.

We must have sounded like a herd of goats on their way to a feed trough the way we tromped down the stairs. I was afraid we'd wake up Miss Janice, even with her room as secluded from the main part of the house as it was. But we were hungry girls with a lot of gossip to share, and this hour of the night was ours to spend how we wanted, regardless of tomorrow's consequences.

We entered the kitchen and soon the table was piled with meat and cheese and dips, a left-over fruit platter, half eaten pies, and bags of potato chips. It was enough to feed an army. We gathered around the table as the remaining house girls, being summoned by text messages, filtered downstairs to join us.

"All right," Cook said, after stuffing a pimento cheese slice in her mouth. "What's happened since book club?"

Lucy began, "Well, I've heard from Larry after I sent him the picture. He said he was certain the guy next to Mr. Dee was indeed Christopher. And there's something else. Larry remembers how the two of them were discussing how Mr. Dee recently found out Christopher was going to be a dad. Christopher apparently denied it. Mr. Dee said he'd never leave his estate to someone who wouldn't care for his own child."

I couldn't swallow my bite. "Do you mean Lydia?"

"It sounds like it." Lucy said. "Christopher is the father."

"She said he booted her to the curb. This is awful. We have to talk with her," I felt horrified.

"Last I heard, she wasn't too happy with us," Mary reminded me. "I was surprised you got her to text back."

"She said Mikey really helped her." I thought about the day in front of the coffee shop. "He bought her clothes and a bear."

"My guess is that Christopher learned Mr. Dee was about to change his will back to Mikey. He wanted to make sure that didn't happen. I still don't understand why, though, if the family money is dried up"

"I know why," I said. "I'm pretty sure the rumors about the gold vein are true. At least Christopher thought so. We found mining equipment in an underground tunnel beneath the church. There was also evidence that his family truly is the owner of that fifteen feet. Mary took a picture of the paper. I think, once it was his, he was banking on the gold mine panning out."

"Call the police. Do it now."

We all looked up to see Miss Janice standing in the doorway. I shivered. She may be small, but she was fierce and the look in her eye now went straight to my bones.

"They tried to pin this on me, did they?" she continued. "Well, I'll show them. Cook, fire up the grill. I'm in the mood for tacos!"

CHAPTER THIRTY

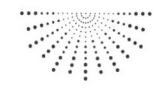

The grandfather clock chimed midnight in admonishment that we were all still awake. Even worse, there was laughter and giggles breaking out, cheese being spilled, and tacos eaten. We would all ignore the time, tonight. The detectives were on their way here and no one was in the least bit sleepy.

While we waited, we hashed out more details. Somewhat mortified, Miss Janice confirmed the bloody handkerchief was the result of a nose bleed in the car. Mary messaged Lydia, who corroborated the bartender's statement that Christopher was the driver of the jeep. She said Mikey arrived to take her to her appointments absolutely furious that he'd had to take the Lincoln because Christopher had swiped his jeep keys.

Mary and Lydia had a good long chat. Cook got involved and promised a knitted baby blanket. In the midst of this, Lydia contacted Dylan (the guy from the dry cleaner's who stood up Mary). Apparently, no-one was sleeping tonight.

At any rate, Lydia begged him to share what he knew. And share he did. A few minutes before the detectives arrived, he sent an unexpected message to Mary.

—I'm sorry I didn't show up at the coffee shop. Dario found out we were meeting and he forbid it. I was told that on behalf of Christopher we were to have nothing to do with anyone from the Thornberry estate. I'd very much like a do-over

That made Mary smile. She wrote back—Possibly. Can you tell me any favors Dario might have done for Christopher?

—I heard there was something about a gas station receipt.

—Why did he do him a favor?

—Christopher said he would pay him once the estate was his.

Several tacos later and finally detectives arrived. The case being so prestigious accounted for the detective getting up out of bed and showing up.

Cook patted my hand and smiled, her eyes twinkling with encouragement. I needed all I could get, because the officer sitting across from me was stern. His badge said Spicer, and he took my statement, which amounted to our experience under the church and what we saw.

On the other side of the room Marguerite sat with Mary, who was faring about the same. The excitement had worn off from earlier and we were both tired.

Detective Spicer looked at me skeptically. "You're saying the cat had his paw on the chemicals."

"On the book page. That's right."

Cook brought me a cup of tea, for which I was so thankful.

"A book of poisons?"

"No. It's actually a family book. Inside, they described their process to find gold. It made me think of Christopher's profile page where he said he went to school for nursing, as well as a degree in chemistry."

Detective Spicer arched an eyebrow. "And you went back to the property why?"

"Because we'd heard about gold."

"There wasn't even a gold mine validated there. It was a rumor."

"Correct. But it was a family rumor. And families keep their secrets close." I hugged my mug of tea. "At any rate, that's how we found the ester bottles."

"Great." The detective did not look like he thought it was all that great. "Do you have anything else you want to share?"

"Mr. Dee found out about Lydia's pregnancy and was ready to change his will, returning Mikey to a proper heir. Christopher knew he was running out of time, so he spiked Mr. Dee's drink. To cover his tracks, he posed as Mikey to the casual onlooker, as well as acquired a receipt from a restaurant. And, as further insurance, he asked Dario to put the receipt in Miss Janice's suit pocket."

"You've got this all wrapped up, do you?" The detective grinned.

I shrugged. "Pretty close. We have the photos and texts you can read."

"I'll tell you what, you are close. Too close. But you didn't need to worry. We have most of the loose ends already tied up behind the scenes. Although I will be visiting Dylan and Larry. Again."

"Again?" I squealed.

His lip lifted in amusement. "Like I said, you didn't need to worry. We always get our man. That's all I'm telling you." He glanced at his partner. "You about finished?"

The other detective nodded. After just a minute more, they started toward the doorway.

As Detective Spicer passed Miss Janice, he paused and rested a hand on her shoulder. "I'm sorry this has been so hard on you. I hope it comforts you that you're in the clear now."

"In the clear? I should have hoped so," Miss Janice snapped back.

The detective narrowed his eyes. "We also obtained a statement from the newspaper. They received a message a few days ago asking about the identity of someone who posted a very specific personal ad. One that seems to have been directed at you."

"Yes." She thrust her shoulders back. "And?"

"And the payment for the ad went through as credit, which made it very easy to track the person down. It's a small thing, but the small things are what trip people up. The bad guy wasn't too smart after all."

"And?" Miss Janice asked again. "I hardly think I should be left hanging when the whole town thinks I did this."

"And right this minute Christopher is in one interview room, and Dario in the other, and Jackson in the last. Let's just say the last two are squealing like pigs. Tomorrow's newspaper already has the headline written to exonerate you."

"Are you saying you didn't need help from my girls?"

Detective Spicer's gaze wandered around the room. "You are lucky to have people like this in your corner."

"Indeed I am," she agreed.

"You all sleep well now," he said and followed his partner to the foyer. The door was already open, held by Butler.

"Well, that takes the cake," Miss Janice said. "I'm about to be in the newspapers yet again."

"You're famous!" Mary said.

Miss Janice rolled her eyes. "I'm off to bed. Thank you ladies for all you've done. I say we all head to bed and try to get some rest. I've heard the plumbers are returning tomorrow."

A groan rose from all of us.

"You girls shush," Marguerite said. "We'll be fine, Miss Janice. We'll see you in the morning."

Miss Janice went up the stairs, with a trail of girls following behind her. I was ready to hit the hay myself. I stared at the scattered mugs of tea.

"You need any help?" I asked Cook, trying to hide a yawn.

"You go on," Cook said, shooing me. "Marguerite and I will have a little nightcap and then clean up."

Thankful, I went into the study where I rescued Hank from the cushion. He allowed me to carry him like a heavy bag of beans.

As I came out in the hallway, I heard singing, interrupted by Marguerite's sharp retort. I paused outside the doorway to listen.

"There's no doubting this feeling," Cook warbled, sounding like she was on her second nightcap.

"Don't do it," Marguerite warned.

Cook taunted her by raising her voice several decibels. "I mean this craaaazy feeling."

I winced. It was like being near a dentist drill.

Marguerite must have thought so as well. "That Johnny-boy's addled your brains, I swear. Just listen to you."

"And yooooou make me feel soo good."

"Giving you the IQ of a walnut. Nothing about this song is making *me* feel very good."

I peeked inside the cracked door and saw Cook point the toe of her fluffy slipper at Marguerite. "And youhooo, you are the reason for my feeling."

Marguerite picked up a dish towel and tossed it at her. Cook jumped up, grabbed Marguerite's hand, and started to dance around her. Marguerite remained seated with a look of horror.

"And together weeeeee will make this work. We belong together." Cook went in for the gusto, eyes shut, head back, mouth open wide. The sound was impressive in its volume.

Marguerite rolled her eyes and shook her head. Slowly she rose to her feet. She stared at Cook, and Cooks eyelids popped open.

In the next moment, Marguerite had her arm slung around Cook's neck. Their heads pressed together, and she joined in to the chorus. "We belong together, and always will be. Forever together, you and me."

AFTERWORD

Thank you for reading Poisonous Paws. I appreciate the reviews so much.

Be sure to catch the next installment in Selling Sabotage! Have a great day.

Printed in Great Britain
by Amazon